One by one the t[...]s and then drifted off to their rooms. Nancy, Bess, and George found the large room they were sharing on the second floor. "Too bad," Bess said, gazing out the window at rolling countryside. "I peeked in Rhonda and Rachel's room across the hall, and they have an ocean view."

"Wouldn't you know it," grumbled George.

"Now, give the Selkirks a break," Bess said. "They can't help being rich. And Rhonda may be a bit spoiled, but Rachel's okay."

"You know," Nancy said, "I didn't tell you guys about this before, but in the airport I noticed this one shifty-looking guy on the Sydney flight. I swear Rachel recognized him as we drove off—and she looked pretty upset."

"Did Rhonda see him?" asked Bess.

"That was odd, too," Nancy said. "Rhonda shook her head at Rachel without even looking to see if she knew the guy. It was like she knew he was there, but didn't want to admit it."

Nancy Drew
Mystery Stories

Available from Simon & Schuster

NANCY DREW® 168

THE BIKE TOUR MYSTERY

CAROLYN KEENE

Aladdin Paperbacks
New York London Toronto Sydney Singapore

This book is a work of fiction. Any references to historical events, real people, or real locales are used fictitiously. Other names, characters, places, and incidents are the product of the author's imagination, and any resemblance to actual events or locales or persons, living or dead, is entirely coincidental.

First Aladdin Paperbacks edition September 2002

Copyright © 2002 by Simon & Schuster, Inc.

ALADDIN PAPERBACKS
An imprint of Simon & Schuster
Children's Publishing Division
1230 Avenue of the Americas
New York, NY 10020

Printed in the United States of America

10 9 8 7 6

NANCY DREW and NANCY DREW MYSTERY STORIES are registered trademarks of Simon & Schuster, Inc.

Library of Congress Control Number: 2002100862

ISBN 0-7434-3763-2

Contents

1

Welcome to Ireland

"And how long do you intend to stay in Ireland, Miss, uh . . ." The passport clerk glanced briefly over the U.S. passport in front of him. "Miss Drew?"

"About two weeks," Nancy Drew replied. "I'm going on a cross-country cycling tour."

The clerk's green eyes flicked up to glance at the tall, willowy American teenager with red-blond hair. He smiled. "Well, I'm hoping your legs are strong, then. Ireland's got a powerful lot of hills, especially here in the West."

Nancy smiled back. "Oh, I think I'm up to it. I've been training for a few weeks, with my friend George." She pointed to the athletic-looking dark-haired girl standing in line behind her.

"Well, best of luck to you." He flipped her passport

1

to a blank page, punched it with his stamping machine, and handed it back. "Next!"

Nancy walked past the desk and joined her other friend, Bess Marvin, who had already passed through the immigration interview. "Isn't it exciting, Nancy?" Bess said. "Everyone here is so friendly and warm."

Nancy suppressed a smile. She was used to Bess's quick assumptions, but they still amused her. "You can't judge a whole population by one official," she said. "But yes, the Irish people are known for being very friendly."

"I can't wait to get on that bike and start whizzing through the countryside," Bess went on, twirling a lock of her blond hair. "Those pictures in the tour company's brochure made everything look so picturesque. Thatched-roof cottages, woolly white sheep, crumbling stone walls . . ."

"Just don't expect leprechauns, shamrocks, and pots of gold at the end of every rainbow," warned Nancy with a giggle.

George Fayne strode toward them, hitching her carry-on bag onto her shoulder. "Well, that's over. Now on to the baggage claim. We'd better grab a cart—Bess brought a mountain of luggage."

Bess stuck out her tongue at George, who was not only her close friend, but also her cousin. "I didn't bring that much!" she protested. "After all, we'll be here two weeks. And we need at least two outfits per day. You can't expect me to go to dinner wearing the same clothes I've been bicycling in all day."

"Why not? That's what I plan to do," George said.

"Then remind me not to sit near you at the dinner table. Whew!" Bess waved a hand in front of her nose.

The three girls trooped through a pair of glass doors to the swarming baggage claim area. Most of the bags from their flight had already circled into sight on the luggage carousel. Nancy quickly spotted her black suitcase, thanks to the neon green ribbon she had knotted onto its handle. George's big purple duffel bag was next to it. The two girls lifted their bags off the conveyor belt.

Bess frowned as she began to search through the mounds of bags already removed from the carousel. "Two tan suitcases, just like my carry-on. Oh, there's one!" She sprang over to the edge of the carousel and checked the ID tags on the suitcase. "No, sorry. That belongs to someone else. It's just like mine, though."

"Bess, you'll never learn," George groaned. "You buy this year's trendiest luggage style, and everyone on the flight has the same bags you do."

"I always find them eventually," Bess shot back. "It isn't my fault you're in such a hurry."

"The rest of our tour group *is* waiting for us," Nancy reminded Bess. She exchanged wry glances with George. The three girls traveled together often. The scenario was familiar by now.

As Bess scurried off to inspect another tan suitcase, Nancy was jostled from behind. Ever alert, she shifted around to see who it was.

A broad-shouldered man in a black wool overcoat was shoving through the crowd milling around the neighboring carousel. Something about his heavy-browed, tight-mouthed face made Nancy uneasy. Eyes trained on someone ahead in the foot traffic, he seemed in a great hurry.

As he hoisted a duffel to his shoulder, Nancy idly noted that the little finger was missing from his left hand. With the instincts of a trained detective, she glanced at the electronic sign above the adjacent carousel, noting that its flight was from Sydney, Australia.

"Found them!" Nancy heard Bess announce. She turned to see Bess stacking her carry-on atop two larger suitcases. "And we don't need a cart, George—my new suitcases have wheels on them."

"So you do learn from experience." George grinned. "After I've toted your heavy bags down so many long terminals!"

"We still have to pass through customs inspection," Nancy reminded her friends, nodding toward a final set of doors.

"Ooh—will they open our cases?" Bess asked, looking concerned as she maneuvered her tower of luggage toward the doors.

"Probably not—but they do perform random checks of passengers' bags," Nancy said. "I think they zero in on people who look suspicious."

As they passed through the swinging doors, Nancy noticed one passenger who'd been called over to the customs official's table—the man in the black overcoat from the Australian flight. And from the expression on his face, Nancy guessed he wasn't happy about being inspected.

Nancy's curiosity was piqued. Her father, prominent River Heights attorney Carson Drew, often told her she was a natural detective. Back home, she'd worked on several important cases. Even though she was on vacation, she couldn't help being intrigued by shady activity.

Bess and George were hurrying ahead toward the exit doors. The Irish customs officials were apparently not interested in checking the three American girls' bags. And Nancy eagerly followed them, looking forward to meeting the rest of their cycling tour group.

Emerging from the customs area, the girls looked around for their tour leader. They spotted him easily—a twentysomething man with curly brown hair, holding up a cardboard sign reading, MCELHENEY TOURS. They walked over to him. "Mr. Prendergast?" George asked.

The young man smiled. "Call me Bob," he said in

an American accent. "Are you the girls from River Heights?"

"Yes—I'm George Fayne. And here's Nancy Drew and Bess Marvin." George gestured toward her friends.

Bob shook hands all around. "Glad to meet you. Did you have a good flight?" The girls nodded their heads. "Good. Some of the other folks are here—let me introduce you."

He led the girls over to a small waiting area with vinyl couches. Three other newly arrived passengers were slumped on the seats, surrounded by suitcases and looking weary from their flights.

"We've got the whole American contingent now," Bob said cheerfully, parking Bess's stacked bags for her. "Everyone, here's George Fayne, Nancy Drew, and Bess Marvin, from River Heights. Girls, this is Carl Thompson—he's from Boston. College professor, right, Carl?"

A large man with a bushy brown beard and twinkling dark eyes stood up. "Assistant professor in chemistry—but thanks for the promotion, Bob."

"Anytime," Bob replied brightly. "And here are Jim and Natalie de Fusco, from California."

"North or south?" Nancy asked as she shook hands with the young, suntanned, blond couple.

"Near San Diego," Jim de Fusco said. "I work construction, and Natalie manages a surf shop."

"And you're missing surf season?" asked George.

"Truth is," Natalie admitted, "when you live near sunny beaches year-round, you get tired of them. Believe it or not, we hope for chilly, rainy weather every day."

"Great," Bob declared. "Because this is Ireland, and I can promise it will rain. Now, if you'll excuse me—I've got two other tour members coming out of customs any minute." He darted away.

"Does it really rain so often here?" Bess wondered, looking out the airport window at a clear blue sky.

Carl gave a philosophical shrug. "Sure. But look on the bright side—that's why western Ireland's one of the greenest places on earth."

"I think rain's refreshing on a bicycle ride," George said. "Who wants hot weather when you're pedaling up and down hills?"

"I'm with you on that," chuckled Carl.

"I'm surprised that we have an American tour guide," Nancy remarked to the group.

"Bob told me his specialty is cycling, not Ireland," Jim said. "But he's led several groups around here the past couple of years. He says it's a great country for cycling—not too many mountains, and lots of sight-seeing."

"Oh, I can't wait," Bess said.

A moment later, Bob returned with a striking pair

of girls, one redhead and one brunette, both nearly six feet tall. "Here we are," Bob said. "I'd like you to meet Rhonda and Rachel Selkirk." He repeated everyone's names for the newcomers.

"G'day, all," brunette Rhonda said in a broad Australian accent. "Glad to be here at last. That flight from Sydney seemed to take forever—I'm really knackered."

"Sorry, but I have to ask," Bess said. "You two look so much alike. Are you twins or sisters?"

Red-haired Rachel laughed. "Just sisters. But don't worry—we get asked that all the time."

"Now, everybody, collect your things and we can load them into the van," Bob said. "Terry, our driver, has got it parked right out at the curb."

As the tour group began to gather their gear, a porter came up behind the Selkirks, pushing a cart. On it were a few handsome leather suitcases and two large, narrow packing crates that were curved at both ends.

"Whoa—you brought your own bikes?" George exclaimed. "Wasn't that expensive?"

Rachel looked vague. "I guess so," she said. "But we prefer to ride our bikes rather than what the tour company provides. Not to knock your bikes," she added apologetically to Bob.

"These bikes were custom-made for us," Rhonda added, tossing her shoulder-length brown hair.

8

"Seemed a shame not to use them, eh?"

"Those girls either are pro cyclists or they're awfully rich," Bess whispered to Nancy as they followed the others out the terminal's exit doors.

"Probably the latter," Nancy replied softly, "judging from that expensive luggage. And pro cyclists aren't likely to join a tour like this."

"If they've had bikes custom-made, they must really be into cycling," George muttered, joining her friends. "And they look like they're in top shape. I'll bet they're super cyclists."

Nancy laughed. "And you're already determined to outride them," she teased her friend. "George, this isn't a race. We're just here to get some exercise and see Ireland at a leisurely pace."

George nodded, but she kept studying the tall, athletic-looking Selkirks.

The group headed for a cherry red van parked at the curb, with MCELHENEY TOURS painted on the sides. A rumpled Irishman with a gloomy expression stood by the open side doors. "This is Terry O'Leary," Bob announced. "He'll drive your luggage from one night's hotel to the next while you cycle along. He's also the guy who can repair your bikes— so be nice to him."

Terry flashed a gap-toothed smile, but Nancy wasn't convinced it was genuine.

The tour members piled their luggage beside the

McElheney van, then followed Bob to a sleek black minibus parked just behind it.

Waiting to board the passenger van, Nancy sensed a commotion on the sidewalk behind her. Out of the corner of her eye she recognized a black overcoat. It was the man with the missing finger from the Sydney flight!

Then a connection clicked in her brain.

Nancy peered inside the van. The Australian girls were sitting inside. Rhonda was rooting in her purse for something.

Then Rachel looked out through the window—and spotted the man in the black overcoat.

And Nancy could swear Rachel froze in fear.

2

The Gang's All Here

"Rhonda, wasn't that—?" Rachel began, poking her sister in the arm.

But Rhonda, barely looking up, cut her off. "Don't be silly, Rache," she said, tossing her thick brown hair. "We've only been in Ireland an hour. How could you possibly recognize anyone?"

Nancy watched Rachel's expression as she sank back in her seat. She didn't look at all convinced, Nancy thought.

Climbing onto the bus, Nancy told herself to put the incident out of her mind. *You've been working on too many mysteries lately,* she scolded herself. *You imagine crimes wherever you look. Just relax and enjoy your vacation.*

With everyone aboard, the minibus pulled away,

After navigating the tangle of roads around Shannon Airport, they were soon rolling across open country-side. Nancy's first impression was an overwhelming sensation of green.

"So that's why green is always used to symbolize Ireland," George said, gazing out the window. "I've never seen such an intense color."

"Look at that old stone cottage," Bess exclaimed, pointing. "Isn't it charming?"

"There sure is a lot of farmland around here," said Natalie de Fusco, across the aisle.

"Yeah, but what tiny farms," George said. "There's the next farmhouse already. And I don't see any big red barns like back home."

"What I love are the crooked stone walls between the fields," Jim said. "Do you know, they don't even use mortar to make those walls? They just pick up stones from the fields and fit them in place. But they're remarkably strong—some of those walls are well over a hundred years old."

Natalie rolled her eyes. "Trust you, Jim, to know all the construction details."

The bus curved around winding roads until, less than an hour later, they pulled up to a large rambling house, a quirky pile of eaves and gables in warm yellow stone. "Wow, what is this—someone's country manor?" Bess asked, impressed.

George scanned the tour itinerary Bob had passed

out to the group. "It says this is our hotel for the first night—Ballyrae House. We're in a town called Lahinch, on the western coast."

"Terry has already arrived, I see," Bob said, standing up and spotting the red van in a side lot. "Your luggage will be taken up to your rooms. In the meantime, let's gather for a quick meeting."

Bob led the way through a marble entry hall and into a wood-paneled parlor, where a young couple sat in a pair of leather armchairs. "Ah, I see our final two cyclists are here," Bob said. "Folks, meet Derek Thorogood and Camilla Collins, just off the ferry from England."

As Derek and Camilla shook hands and learned the names of their tour companions, Nancy noticed Bess's dazzled expression. Even Nancy had to admit that Derek was handsome, with his shaggy dark hair, lazy gray eyes, and clean-cut features.

"Here goes Bess with another crush," George whispered in Nancy's ear. "I bet she hasn't even noticed that Derek brought a girlfriend with him."

"I heard that," Bess muttered, whirling around. "And just because they travel together doesn't mean they're boyfriend and girlfriend."

"No, but I'd say it's a pretty good clue," George shot back. "That and the fact that Camilla's draped herself all over his shoulder."

"Relax, girls," Nancy broke in. "Time will tell

whether or not Derek is 'available.' And even if he isn't, who cares? This seems like a great bunch of people. I'm looking forward to riding with them—all of them."

As a waiter passed around cold drinks, Bob asked the members of the tour group to sit down. "This is probably a good time to go over the protocols for our tour," he announced. "You all have copies of the itinerary I passed out."

Several members of the group waved their itineraries in the air.

"Hang on to these," Bob advised. "They'll be your bibles for the next ten days. There's a page for each day, which we'll supplement each morning with a detailed road map of that day's route. The itinerary tells where our lunch stop will be—usually a historic site. I've typed up a brief paragraph describing each lunch sight, but you can use your own guidebooks for more details."

"Got mine," Carl said, holding up a thick paperback book. From the dog-eared pages, Nancy guessed Carl had done plenty of pre-trip research.

"We also describe other sights you'll pass along the way," Bob continued. "Some of you may want to stop and explore. Others may be more interested in keeping up a good cycling pace. You're free to go as you please."

Natalie de Fusco frowned. "But aren't we going to ride as a group?"

Bob shook his head. "After a few years of running these cycling tours, I've learned that that doesn't work. You're all at different levels of cycling ability. Some people may want to ride forty or fifty miles in a day. Others may get tired after fifteen or twenty."

"That'll be me," Camilla Collins admitted. Noting the English girl's fair skin, manicured nails, and carefully styled brown hair, Nancy guessed she wasn't the outdoors type.

"Well, we've designed the tour to work for all levels," Bob reassured them. "As often as possible, I've plotted out a longer route and a shorter route for each day's ride. And if you want to quit after the morning ride, Terry can drive you from the lunch stop to that evening's hotel."

"What if you want to sleep late in the morning?" Jim de Fusco asked, winking at Natalie.

"Well, then Terry can drive you to catch up with the tour at the lunch stop," Bob said, with a sideways grin. "But seriously, I wouldn't advise that—it's always better to ride in the morning, when the air is cooler and clearer."

Nancy raised her hand. "It sounds like we're going to be all over the place," she remarked. "How will you keep track of everybody—for safety's sake?"

"Glad you asked, Nancy," Bob said. "Each morning when I hand out the day's maps, I'll also give a cell phone to each couple of riders. Both Terry and I are programmed into the speed dial, so you can call us anytime. If you get lost or need a repair, we'll find you. Terry can get there faster, of course, since he's got the van."

"You won't be in the van?" Rhonda asked.

"No, I'll be on my bike, riding along with you all," Bob explained. "I'll try to catch up with every group at some time throughout the day. And, of course, we'll all meet at lunch."

"You said 'each couple of riders'—are we assigned to ride in pairs?" Derek asked, his gaze flickering for an instant toward Camilla. Recalling Camilla's comment, Nancy guessed he was a more serious cyclist than his girlfriend.

Bob shook his head. "I hope you'll ride with different people each day," he said. "That's the great thing about riding with a group—getting to know one another. Of course, the really fast riders may not care to stay too long with the slower riders. So we'll be flexible. The only rule is, always ride with at least one other person, and always have a phone with each group. Beyond that, you can sort it out for yourselves."

A satisfied murmur arose from the crowd. "Sounds like they've thought out all the problems," George remarked to Nancy and Bess.

"Well, I'm glad I won't have to keep up with you two all the time," Bess said, sighing in relief.

Nancy chuckled. "You should have followed George's training plan for the past month, Bess. You'd be in a lot better cycling shape now."

"I know, I know," Bess admitted. "But it seemed so boring at the time."

"Well, don't complain to me if every muscle in your body is sore tomorrow night," George teased her cousin.

Bob Prendergast lifted his voice above the crowd. "Everybody, listen up! We've got several bikes parked outside." He gestured toward a pair of French doors leading to a side terrace. "I know Rhonda and Rachel brought their own, but the rest of you have to choose a bike to ride throughout the tour. So can we step outside?"

Everyone eagerly jumped to their feet and went outdoors. Terry O'Leary stood beside a row of gleaming ten-speed bikes. Their slim aluminum tube frames were painted a bright variety of colors.

"Dibs on the powder blue one," Bess called.

"Better try it out first," warned Terry O'Leary. "Forget the color—you want one that'll suit your height and arm reach."

Bess, blushing with embarrassment, obediently swung her leg over the bike so that Terry could measure how her feet hit the pedals. "Seat's a bit high yet," he muttered. He whipped a hexagonal wrench out of the pocket of his grubby corduroy pants and lowered the seat post. Next he adjusted the angle of the handlebars. "Now it'll do, miss," he said gruffly. Bess pushed off, tottering, on the blue bicycle.

The rest of the group crowded around the various bikes to make their choices. Nancy selected a dark green bicycle, while George settled on a bronze-colored one. "These are good bikes—not as good as mine at home, but still very rideable," George said approvingly.

Rhonda Selkirk spoke up from the terrace wall where she sat with her sister. "Funny how heavy those aluminum frames look, now that I'm used to titanium," she said casually.

George shot Rhonda a glance that wasn't all that friendly. "The weight difference can't be more than a pound or two," she said.

"True," Rhonda replied agreeably. "Still, every ounce matters when you're climbing a hill."

"Remember, these are touring bikes, not dirt bikes," Bob spoke above the hubbub. "Those narrow tires don't have thick treads, so they puncture easily—you may get flats. I'll give you all tire repair kits so you can put on a temporary patch, pump up the mended tire, and ride on. Then Terry can put a new inner tube and tire on that night."

"Better still, don't ride over any nails or broken glass," Rhonda joked.

Bob grinned. "That, too," he said. "And one more thing: You Americans, don't forget to ride on the left-hand side of the road!"

One by one the tour members claimed bikes and then drifted off to their rooms. Nancy, Bess, and George found the large room they were sharing on the second floor. "Too bad," Bess said, gazing out the window at rolling countryside. "I peeked in Rhonda and Rachel's room across the hall, and they have an ocean view."

"Wouldn't you know it," grumbled George.

"Now, give the Selkirks a break," Bess said. "They can't help being rich. And Rhonda may be a bit spoiled, but Rachel's okay."

"You know," Nancy said, "I didn't tell you guys about this before, but in the airport I noticed this one shifty-looking guy on the Sydney flight. I swear Rachel recognized him as we drove off—and she looked pretty upset."

"Did Rhonda see him?" asked Bess.

"That was odd, too," Nancy said. "Rhonda shook her head at Rachel without even looking to see if she knew the guy. It was like she knew he was there, but didn't want to admit it."

George touched Nancy's forehead as if testing for fever. "You need some time off, Nan," she said with a grin. "You're getting a little paranoid. Anyway, it happened back at Shannon—I bet we never run into that character again."

An hour later, the girls went down to meet the group for dinner. "Now we'll get the view," Nancy said as they entered the dining room. A huge picture window on the west wall showed a brilliant sunset sparkling over the Atlantic.

Rachel Selkirk joined the River Heights girls at the window. "What a ripper of a view!" she said. "I'm so glad we chose to do this cycling trip. You can really get in touch with the landscape when you ride through it instead of just staring out the window of a car."

Nancy was just about to reply when she heard a slither and a soft thud behind her. She whirled around to check out what had happened.

There lay Rhonda Selkirk, collapsed in a heap on the dining room floor.

3

A Wee Bit of Trouble

Derek Thorogood jumped up from where he had been sitting, next to Rhonda. "I was talking to her, and she just got all woozy. She started swaying about in her chair, then she tipped over."

Everyone in the dining room broke out in worried murmurs. Almost as one, they rose from their seats and gathered around the spot where Rhonda lay sprawled on the carpet.

Bob Prendergast pushed through the onlookers. "Rhonda?" He knelt quickly at her side and laid a hand against her cheek.

"Her breathing seems to be okay," Bess pointed out. She'd worked at Nancy's side often enough to have a pretty good idea of what to look for in an emergency. "Does her skin feel cold and clammy, or hot and feverish?"

"Neither," Bob said shortly. "Still, I think we'd better call a doctor. I'll go ask the innkeeper to phone a local physician." He searched the ring of faces around him for Rhonda's sister. "Rachel—everything will be okay."

Rachel, looking numb with shock, gave a tense little nod. Bob jumped up and jogged out of the dining room in search of the inn's owners.

Some instinct made Nancy take a careful look around at the circled tour group. To her surprise, she saw that Derek Thorogood was quietly lifting a camera up to his face. Could he really be planning to take a picture of Rhonda lying unconscious? Why would anyone be so intrusive?

But before she could do anything, Natalie de Fusco's voice broke in. "You were sitting with her, Derek—what happened?" she asked.

All eyes turned on him. Derek swiftly slid the camera under his blazer. He pointed to the glass of orange soda sitting on the table at Rhonda's suddenly empty place. "She had just taken a few sips of that Orange Squash," he said, and his dark eyebrows knit in concern.

Nancy heard a little gasp from behind her. She wheeled around to see Rachel, her face completely pale beneath its sprinkling of freckles. "But . . . but that was *my* soda!" she cried out.

Nancy gripped the back of the chair next to her. She didn't want to jump to conclusions, but *if* the orange soda was responsible for Rhonda's blackout—then had it been intended for Rhonda to drink, or for Rachel?

As the group rallied around Rachel, Nancy sank back on a nearby table, her mind racing. Glancing at her watch, she did a swift calculation. Rhonda couldn't have been in the room longer than five minutes before Nancy arrived. Most poisons and drugs take at least twenty minutes to take effect. Of the ones that work immediately, most cause vomiting, convulsions, or gastric pain. But Nancy could see Rhonda lying there on the red-patterned rug—not writhing, not thrashing around, not even breathing very hard.

Nancy rose to her feet and began to move toward the suspect glass of soda, careful not to let anyone notice her.

But Carl Thompson got there first. He picked up the half-full glass, raised it to his nose, and sniffed. "No unusual odor," the professor remarked. "If the drink had been laced with cyanide, it would smell like almonds."

Nancy exchanged a quick glance with Bess. Maybe she wouldn't have to reveal her identity as a detective after all.

"Do you really think anyone would put cyanide in her drink?" Natalie asked.

Carl shrugged. "I'm not a detective—just a chemist," he said. "But if something in the glass caused her to pass out, it was either a poison like cyanide or some drug—a barbiturate powder, maybe. A drug wouldn't have a distinguishing scent, however."

Trying to act like an ordinary bystander so as not to make anyone feel uncomfortable, Nancy asked Carl, "How would you find out? Could you run a chemical test of the remaining soda?"

Carl smiled. "Well, I'm no traveling lab. But I could probably improvise. With a few household chemicals, I could run some preliminary tests."

"We don't need testing yet," Bob Prendergast broke in, rejoining the group. "There's a physician driving over from the next town to look at Rhonda. Let's wait for his diagnosis. This could be a simple medical situation—a reaction to some medication, or something like that. Meanwhile, could someone fetch a blanket? If Rhonda's blood pressure's dropped, she needs to stay warm."

As though relieved to have something definite to do, the members of the tour bustled around. Nancy took advantage of the stir to draw Bob aside. "Did you contact the police?" she asked.

Bob's eyes darted nervously sideways. "Well, uh, no, not yet. I don't see any need to make a fuss. Rhonda wouldn't want the police involved."

"How can you know that?" Nancy asked.

Bob flinched. "It would be a violation of the Selkirks' privacy," he explained. "And I promised them—" He choked off what he was going to say, casting his eyes downward.

"If I were in their situation, I'd want the police called," Nancy said gently.

Bob's eyes flew up to meet hers. "What do you know about their situation?" he challenged her.

Suddenly, Nancy heard a shattering sound from behind. She whirled around.

The glass of orange soda had been knocked off the table where Carl had so carefully set it aside. A puddle of sticky orange liquid was soaking into the red-patterned carpet, oozing around a few big shards of glass.

Terry O'Leary was already on his knees, mopping up the spill with a pile of paper napkins. "Sorry— clumsy me," he muttered. He plucked glass shards up with his fingers and dropped them into the nearest waste bin, then scrunched up a handful of soggy orange napkins and threw them away.

Nancy clenched her fists at her sides. Now they'd never be able to have that liquid tested!

Nancy caught George's eye and jerked her head upward, indicating the need to talk privately. George nodded and glanced at Bess. Bess looked back at Nancy and fluttered her eyelids in reply.

Nancy backed quietly out of the dining room, hoping no one would notice her going. She trotted up the staircase to the girls' room. A moment later, George came in, followed soon after by Bess.

Nancy was tense with anger and disappointment. "Terry O'Leary spilled Rhonda's glass of soda," she fumed. "Now we'll never learn what may have been in it. If I could even get my hands on one piece of glass, there might have been enough soda on it to test."

"It's a tough break—no pun intended—but accidents do happen," Bess said.

Nancy's blue eyes flashed. "I'm not so sure it was an accident. What if Terry *meant* to spill that soda? He heard Carl say he was going to test it."

"Why would Terry want to prevent Carl from testing the soda?" George asked.

"I'm not sure," Nancy admitted, "but I got the distinct impression that Bob wasn't eager to call in the police. And Terry does work for Bob."

"You think Terry and Bob have something to do with Rhonda's passing out?" Bess looked amazed.

Nancy sighed and shrugged. "It's possible. One thing's for sure: Something fishy is going on here. I get the sense there's something about Rhonda and Rachel that we don't know. And this mix-up with the soda bothers me."

"Maybe we should find out more about Derek,"

George said. "He was right next to Rhonda at the table. He had a perfect opportunity to slip something in her drink, didn't he?"

Bess flushed. "How dare you accuse Derek of doing anything wrong!"

George blew out an impatient little breath. "Come on, Bess! Just because you think the guy is gorgeous doesn't mean he's innocent."

Bess glared at her cousin. "It's not just because he's gorgeous. If he had poisoned Rhonda, why would he point out to everybody that she'd just drunk the soda? He would've tried to hide it if he'd been messing with her drink."

"You've got a point, Bess," Nancy said. "All the same, we can't rule him out. I think he was just about to snap a photo of Rhonda while she was lying there. How rude is that? I'd like to know a little more about Derek Thorogood myself."

"You bet," George chimed in. "I mean, he came with Camilla, but he's been hovering around Rhonda and Rachel ever since we arrived. What gives?"

Bess rolled her eyes. "Maybe he's just being friendly. There's no crime in that."

"I'm not saying he's a criminal—I'd just like to know more about him," Nancy said. "And that goes for everybody on this tour. All three of us must keep our eyes and ears open. Now, let's go back downstairs before anyone misses us. Maybe the doctor's here."

She pushed open the door to their room and stepped out in the passageway, casually tucking her hair behind her ears. A movement down the hall caught her eye.

A few yards away, Derek Thorogood crouched in a narrow cranny, hunched over something in his right hand. He was talking quickly and softly to himself. Sensing Nancy's presence, he froze against the wall.

Nancy's sharp eyes picked up the gleam of a tiny electronic device in Derek's hand. It looked like a tape recorder!

Derek thrust the device hastily into his pocket and jumped up. A glib smile spread over his handsome features. "Oh, Nancy, I came up to find you. Thought you might like to know—all's well after all. Rhonda came to, just after you left. Seems none the worse for her scare, thank goodness."

"Well, that's a relief," Nancy said in a guarded tone of voice.

"The doctor never came, but Rhonda swears it was nothing. No medical condition, she's not on any medicines, nothing of that sort. So it was probably an allergic reaction to something in the soda." He blithely waved his hand. "Or maybe jet lag. Anyway, they're about to serve dinner. Where are your two friends?" He looked over Nancy's shoulder.

"They came up to . . . use the bathroom," Nancy said.

"You mean the 'loo.'" Derek smiled and began to guide Nancy toward the stairs. "I'm making it my mission to teach you Americans the local lingo, you know."

"I appreciate it," Nancy said, flashing him a smile. She had to agree with Bess: Derek Thorogood *was* good-looking, and charming, too. But she still didn't trust him.

The low-beamed dining room rang with chatter as Nancy and Derek entered. Nancy glimpsed Rhonda and Rachel at a table with the de Fuscos, looking as if nothing had happened. Derek led Nancy to a table near the picture window. "Well, that was enough excitement for one evening, I can tell you," Camilla said, smiling up at Nancy.

"Yes, indeed," Nancy replied. She took a seat next to Carl Thompson.

Derek rubbed his hands together and began to back away from the table. "Well, I'll just leave those other seats open for Beth and Jo, shall I?"

"Bess and George," Nancy corrected him. "But they can find other seats. Like Bob said, we should all mingle and get to know one another." She patted the chair beside her for Derek to sit down.

"Yes, yes—well, all the more reason why I should sit somewhere else. Right, Camilla?" And before she could reply, Derek had gone to join Bob and Terry at a table by the door.

I can still keep an eye on him from here, Nancy thought, shifting her chair slightly. She lifted her menu and began to decide what to order.

But the next time she remembered to look up, as the soup plates were being taken away, she saw that Derek's chair at the table near the door was empty.

4

A Need for Speed

"So what if Derek *did* leave the dining room?" Bess said as the girls talked in their room later.

"Bess, you've got to admit he's acting suspicious," George argued. "First, Nancy saw him try to snap a photo of Rhonda while she was knocked out. Then he was whispering into a tape recorder. Then he steered Nancy to a table away from Rhonda and Rachel so she couldn't ask them any questions."

"And after I sat down, he sat somewhere else so I couldn't ask *him* any questions," Nancy added, tugging a brush through her hair.

"Then he snuck out of the dining room for almost fifteen minutes," George said.

"Maybe he had to finish recording his tape," Bess suggested.

"Yes, but why was he making a tape recording in the first place?" George demanded, pointing her toothbrush accusingly at Bess.

"None of it makes sense yet," Nancy said. "But like I said, we should be alert for the next few days. I can't help thinking Rhonda and Rachel are the key to everything."

"We should ride with them tomorrow," George said, "to keep an eye on them."

Bess raised her eyebrows. "You two can ride with the Selkirks," she said, rolling over on the bed. "Not me. Those girls are as tall and strong as Amazons, plus they have those fancy titanium bikes. There's no way I'd keep up with them."

Nancy fought a yawn. "Well, there's no way I'll keep up with them, either, if I don't get to bed. I didn't sleep much on the plane last night—too excited. On River Heights time, it's only four P.M., but it's ten here and I'm totally zonked. Let's turn in."

"I'll take Rhonda, you take Rachel," George murmured to Nancy the next morning. They glanced over to where the Selkirk sisters stood beside the hotel steps in their high-tech riding gear—snug black knit shorts and zip-up spandex jerseys.

George self-consciously adjusted the legs of her form-fitting blue shorts, bought new for this trip. Her banana yellow jersey was emblazoned with the name of an Italian racing team. Nancy and Bess had opted for ordinary clothes: khaki cotton hiking shorts, roomy T-shirts, and windbreakers.

"You ride with them, and I'll ride with Derek Thorogood," Bess offered. George gave her a sarcastic look. "Well, you said we should watch him, too," Bess said, a twinkle in her eye.

It was a bright, clear morning with a balmy breeze. As the tour group gathered outside the hotel, Bob Prendergast handed out the day's maps, along with plastic water bottles. "Lunch today is a picnic overlooking the Cliffs of Moher," Bob reminded everybody. "Be there by twelve-thirty."

"Or, as we say over here, half-twelve," Derek added, waggling his eyebrows.

Nancy walked her bicycle over to the Selkirks. "Love your matching magenta bikes," she said. "But how do you tell them apart?"

Rachel smiled. "Easy—I've put silver tape on my handlebars, and Rhonda's got black." She pointed to her down-curved handlebars.

Bob Prendergast joined them. "Who's riding with whom today?"

Nancy turned to Rachel. "Could we ride together?" she asked quickly.

Rachel shrugged as she lifted her silver helmet to strap it on. "Sure, why not?"

"Okay, Rachel and Nancy, here's a cell phone for

the day." Bob handed Nancy a bulky, slightly outdated model of cell phone. "Push speed dial one to reach me, speed dial two for Terry."

"I could ride with you, Rhonda," George piped up, standing behind Bob.

"Great, Rhonda and George are a team," Bob said, handing a cell phone to Rhonda. "I'm glad you're mixing partners. Have a good ride!" He bustled off to finish equipping other riders.

Rhonda shot an annoyed look at George. "Hope you don't mind riding fast," she snapped, slinging her black helmet on top of her glossy dark hair. Rhonda swung onto her bike and pushed off, with George scrambling in her wake.

Rachel smiled at Nancy. "I have to confess—I have a serious need for speed myself," she said. "That's why Rhonda and I hoped we could ride together. But I'm willing to give you a go."

"Thanks," Nancy said, fitting on her own helmet. "Don't worry. I like to ride fast, too."

Nancy and Rachel swung out of the hotel parking lot, turning right onto the road that led north. They cycled downhill into Lahinch, its main street lined with shops and restaurants.

"This looks like a popular resort," Nancy shouted to Rachel, who was riding ahead. "I even saw a dive shop back there. Funny, I wouldn't have thought of scuba diving off the coast of Ireland."

Rachel nodded but said nothing.

A moment later, Nancy tried again. "That looks like a good golf course up ahead. Camilla was saying last night that County Clare's a big golf area—lots of famous courses." She paused, fishing for a response. "Do you play golf?"

Rachel shifted in her seat so she could shout to Nancy. "Sorry—don't mean to be unfriendly—but I don't like yabbering and yakking while I'm riding. It interrupts the flow, don't you think?"

Nancy cheerfully replied, "Okay." But she felt crestfallen. She'd hoped to learn some details about Rachel by talking to her. But even more important, she'd hoped to gain Rachel's confidence. Now she was afraid Rachel would write her off as a chatty airhead.

And a chatty airhead who couldn't cycle seriously, Nancy added to herself a few miles farther on. Everything was all right so long as they rode downhill. But just past Lahinch, the road narrowed and began to climb. George's training regimen had improved Nancy's wind, stamina, and leg strength, but she still didn't know how to shift gears on hills like Rachel did.

Nancy stood up on her pedals to gain extra power as she pushed her bike up the challenging slope. Looking ahead, she saw that Rachel was still seated, pedaling rapidly but smoothly.

Nancy fumbled with her gear lever, shifting down so that she could pedal with less resistance. But it was too late—she'd already lost momentum. The distance between her and Rachel lengthened by the second. Nancy gritted her teeth, determined not to ask Rachel to slow down.

Even without turning, Rachel must have sensed that Nancy had fallen way behind. She halted and got off her bike at the top of the hill. Nancy toiled up the last few steep yards, trying hard not to show the exertion.

"Now this is what I call a view," Rachel said as Nancy finally reached her side.

Nancy nodded gamely and pivoted toward the northwest. What she saw made her completely forget her cycling efforts. Stretching ahead before them, for about five miles, was a stretch of spectacular coastal cliffs, their sheer sides ribboned with five layers of different-colored rockface. On the stony ledges nestled huge flocks of puffins and other seabirds. To the left the Atlantic Ocean gleamed and danced.

"Takes your breath away, eh?" Rachel asked.

It took a second for Nancy to realize that Rachel was kidding her. "Oh—so *that's* why I can't breathe," she said, playing along. "And I thought it was from riding up the hill."

Rachel laughed along with her, but Nancy felt

36

embarrassed. "A new bike always takes getting used to," Rachel said tactfully. "Best get a drink and stretch your calves before we go on."

Nancy nodded and dismounted, hardly daring to admit what a relief it was. Leaning her bike against a signpost, she took her water bottle from a bracket on her bike and took a long swig.

"Looks like we still have some uphill riding to do," Rachel said. Crouching down, she ran her fingers through the gravel on the road's edge by Nancy's bike. "What's that out there?" She pointed north, where a few dark islands dotted the sea.

Nancy peered at her map for a moment. "Looks like those are the Aran Islands," she finally decided.

Rachel stood up suddenly. "Well, we should get going." She grabbed her bike and swung up onto the seat. "Ready?"

"As ready as I'll ever be." Nancy stuffed the map in her pocket and jumped on her bike. Rachel was off with a spurt of gravel before Nancy could fit her shoes into the toe clips on her pedals.

The two bikes sped smoothly down the brief slope that followed the hilltop, but soon the road angled upward again. This time, Nancy paid more attention to gear shifting, clicking down to a lower gear each time the pedals began to strain. *Now I've got the hang of it,* she told herself. She kept her eyes trained on the red reflector below Rachel's seat and fought to match Rachel's pace.

Then suddenly everything went wrong. Nancy's front wheel jerked and wobbled. She heard a grating sound on the pavement. The bike began to lean sideways. Nancy squeezed her handbrakes hard.

The red reflector on Rachel's bike whizzed uphill and away.

Nancy hopped off and examined her front wheel. As she feared, the tire was totally flat. Even worse, it looked like the steel rim of the wheel had cut through the rubber treads.

"Rachel!" Nancy called out. The Australian girl was already at the top of the hill, but she circled and coasted back down to Nancy.

"Looks like you've come a cropper," Rachel said as she saw Nancy's flat. "You won't be able to mend it with the patch kit. Better call that Terry bloke and have him pick you up."

With a sigh, Nancy phoned Terry and told him where to find her. As she hung up, Rachel began waving. "Look! Jim, Natalie, and Carl are just down the hill," she said. "You don't mind if I ride with them, do you? I'll leave you the cell."

"That's fine. Terry will be here soon," Nancy said, swallowing her regret.

After the others had ridden away, Nancy rechecked her tire. She frowned. The tread and the inner tube had a long, straight cut in them—not a simple puncture or a jagged rip.

A worrisome thought struck Nancy: Had Rachel done something to the tire at the top of the hill?

Nancy replayed the scene in her mind—Rachel crouched by Nancy's bike, making Nancy gaze out at the ocean and then pore over her map. She'd had time to slash Nancy's tire. But had she done it?

And if she had, why?

"Nancy, stop brooding about that flat," Bess shouted above the music. "You covered the day's route all right after Terry fixed it, didn't you?"

Nancy shook her head. "Yes, I know. Sorry. But it isn't just getting a flat—anybody could get a flat tire. It just seemed so odd—"

Nancy was cut off by the night's entertainment. The musicians finished with a flourish, and wild applause filled the Currach Pub right up to its low, oak-beamed ceiling. The tour was spending the night in Doolin, a fishing village famous for the music pubs along its short main street. Across the room, Nancy glimpsed Rhonda and Rachel, both safe and sound, sitting at a table with Derek and Camilla. *There's no reason to suspect Rachel caused my flat tire*, Nancy scolded herself. *Just because she didn't want to chat while we were riding—and just because she was eager to ride away with other people. She's focused on her cycling, that's all.*

Nancy told herself to stop fretting. After all, when would she hear such delightful music again? Getting into the spirit, she started to stamp her feet with the chorus. Her thigh muscles twinged painfully.

George noticed and giggled. "Don't worry, Nan— I'm sore, too," she whispered. "So much for keeping up with the Selkirks."

Nancy grinned and glanced back over at the Australians' table. Derek was leaning over and whispering in Rhonda's ear, while Camilla, looking oblivious, swayed to the music.

But where had Rachel gone?

Nancy stiffened and looked around. Though the room was crowded, it was small. Despite the noise and the haze of smoke from a peat fire, every cheery corner was visible. And Rachel was nowhere.

Nancy rose uneasily and started to move toward the door as the sea chanty ended. The applause was dying down when she heard an awful clatter outside, followed by a moan of pain.

Dashing outside, Nancy nearly tripped over Rachel, sprawled on the cobbled street with the pub's heavy wooden sign lying beside her.

5

No Thanks

Bob Prendergast came hurrying out the door right behind Nancy. "Go ask the pub owner for some ice, and have him call a doctor," he said, kneeling beside Rachel. His fingers gently probed the side of her forehead, where Nancy could see a small, bloody gash. "And send Terry out."

"Here already, Bob," came Terry's voice from the shadows beside the pub door. Nancy turned to look at him, standing with his hands thrust in the pockets of his baggy corduroys. How had he arrived so fast and so silently? Nancy wondered. Had he come from inside—or was he outside the whole time?

"Fetch the first-aid kit from the van, Terry," Bob said, not looking up.

Nancy hated to leave the scene of the accident,

but she knew it was crucial to get medical help as soon as possible. Luckily, the pub owner had heard the commotion and was already at the doorway. He promised to bring out some ice as soon as he had phoned a physician. "There's no one directly in town," he warned Nancy. "Doolin's not so big as all that. But Dr. Finney lives only a couple miles off— I'll ring him up."

Bess and George joined Nancy as she headed back outside. "Rachel's been knocked out—it looks like the pub sign fell and hit her in the head," she said anxiously.

"Derek was inside the whole time—I know, I was watching him," Bess said, reading Nancy's mind. "Just in case you were wondering."

As they emerged again into the clear, crisp night air, Nancy was relieved to see Rachel beginning to moan and stir. "My head," Rachel murmured. "Wicked pain . . ." Her eyes fluttered open and then squeezed shut again, as if even the dim light from the pub door was too bright.

A curious crowd had begun to spill out of the doorway. Rhonda pushed her way through, glaring. "Can't you all clear off?" she snapped.

"Yes, that's enough now, you lot," the pub owner said. Handing a bag of ice to Nancy, he shooed the gawkers back inside. Bess and George reluctantly followed them.

Rhonda bent over Rachel. "What were you thinking of?" she scolded her sister. "Why did you go outside? You know you shouldn't slip off on your own."

Rachel winced. "Leave off, Rhon," she replied groggily. "Gotta . . . have a life . . ."

"Where does it hurt, Rachel?" Bob asked.

Rachel lifted a hand weakly and touched the top of her skull, on the right side. "Something heavy— out of nowhere—"

Rhonda glimpsed the blood on her sister's forehead and sucked in her breath. "The sign—it really hit you! Give us that ice, Nancy." She started to lift Rachel's head, but Bob stopped her.

"Best not to move her, in case she's had a concussion," he suggested. "Lay the ice against her head from the side and wait for the doctor."

"No doctor!" Rachel burst out with surprising vehemence. "I'm all right." She pushed herself up onto her elbows with a sudden, forceful effort.

"Now, Rachel, it's best to get checked out," Bob said. "With head injuries, you never know."

"Then send the doctor to the hotel," Rachel declared. "I'm not lying here in the gutter anymore. Help me up, Rhon."

Rhonda took her sister's elbow and helped her to her feet. "We'll be all right, Bob," she said. She cast a worried look up and down the shadowy street. "I'll see she stays in bed. Send the doctor along."

Nancy noted Bob's anxious expression. "I could have Terry drive you in the van," he offered. "He should be back any sec." He glanced around, just realizing that Terry hadn't returned.

"No!" Rhonda insisted. She quickly added, "I'll walk her back. It's not far. Fresh air might do her good—better than being jolted in a van."

"I'll be fine," Rachel announced, lifting her chin as she took a wobbly first step. "Not to worry."

Bob stepped back, hands hanging helplessly at his sides. Nancy stood with him, watching, as the sisters moved tentatively down the sloping street toward the inn where the group was staying. An only child herself, Nancy didn't always understand sibling relationships. But she knew enough to see that this one was complicated indeed.

Jim de Fusco popped out of the front door. "Is Rachel okay?" he asked. "We heard she was hurt, but we didn't want to hover."

"I'll go reassure everyone," Bob said. "Nancy, tell Terry I'm inside. And don't stay out too long—the night air's cold, so close to the sea." He ducked back inside the pub.

"What happened?" Jim asked Nancy.

She pointed to the wood sign on the pavement. "Apparently that fell and clonked Rachel on the side of the head."

Jim knelt to inspect the thick slab of wood, carved

in the shape of a wicker-framed one-man boat. "So that's what the pub's named after—a currach fishing boat," he said. He ran his hands over the wood. "Nice carving. Real craftsmanship."

"This makes two accidents in a row," Nancy remarked. "Rhonda passed out last night, and now this with Rachel. If it *was* an accident."

With a professional eye, Jim studied the end of one of the chains from which the sign had hung. "Hard to tell how it happened. This chain link is twisted, like it had torn loose. Maybe the other side was rusted . . ." He picked up its mate, then gave a low whistle. "No, this one's been cut, clean through, like someone hacked it with a saw."

"Let me see." Nancy bent down to examine the two chains. "So once this chain was severed—"

"The other one would eventually break," Jim replied. "It couldn't hold the weight on its own. These chains are pretty thin to carry such a heavy sign. If I'd hung it, I'd have used a thicker chain."

Nancy looked solemnly at Jim. "So possibly someone meant for Rachel to get hurt."

Jim screwed his mouth to the side. "Maybe. I'd sure like to know why the one chain was cut."

"So would I," Nancy said grimly. She swiveled and began to hunt around the pavement. If she could find a discarded hacksaw, or even a pile of iron shavings . . .

Her eyes fell on a patch of white on the ground,

right where Rachel had fallen. She stooped to pick it up. On a crumpled piece of paper was scrawled, "R—Meet me outside—D."

Nancy chewed her lip. Who had written this note? Someone whose name started with "D." Derek Thorogood? He had been sitting at the table with Rachel, Nancy remembered. Why had he needed to see her privately?

She turned to face Jim. "We should let Bob know what we found," she said. "I'll go to the inn to talk to Rhonda and Rachel."

Jim nodded and went back inside. Drawing a steadying breath, Nancy headed down the street toward their inn. She fingered the corner of the note in her pocket. *Think logically*, she reminded herself, like her father had always told her. *Don't make quick assumptions*. For instance, why assume the note was for Rachel? R could just as easily stand for Rhonda. Either girl might have dropped it when she came outside tonight.

The note might have nothing to do with the accident, Nancy mused. But still, it was worth checking out. It was no more puzzling than the other facts in this case so far.

The lilt of music-making coursed through the evening air, only the tune changing as Nancy passed each of the village's pubs in turn. But she was thinking too hard to notice.

Reaching the inn, Nancy marched past the front desk and straight upstairs. With its whitewashed walls and polished plank floors, the inn was more rustic than last night's lodgings, but it was cozy and quiet. The Selkirks' room was at the end of the third-floor hallway. Nancy rapped on their door. "Who is it?" Rhonda called.

"Nancy Drew. I have to talk to you."

After a brief silence, Rhonda called back, "Another time, Nancy. Rachel needs to sleep."

"If she's had a concussion, she should stay awake," Nancy warned. "Are her pupils dilated?"

"Go away!" Rhonda replied.

Then Nancy heard Rachel's low murmur. A moment later, the door opened. Rachel faced her. "Come on in, Nancy," she said. "I am feeling groggy, I must admit, but we can talk."

Nancy glanced at Rachel's pupils, which she was glad to see were normal sized. "How many fingers?" she asked, holding up three fingers.

"I already did all those tests," Rhonda said, leafing through a magazine on the bed. "And it's not like you're a doctor, Nancy."

"No, I'm no doctor," Nancy admitted. She paused, making certain of her own decision. "But I *am* a detective," she revealed.

Rachel's eyes widened. Rhonda slapped shut her magazine. "For real?" Rachel asked.

Nancy nodded. "I'm just an amateur, but I've solved lots of cases. No one on the trip knows, except Bess and George. But I think you need someone to look out for you. Knowing my background, will you let me help?"

Rachel fidgeted. "Thanks, but no thanks, Nancy. It's sweet of you to offer, but we don't need protection. Those were two random accidents."

Nancy raised her eyebrows. "That falling sign may not have been an accident," she said. She told them what she and Jim had discovered.

Rhonda snorted. "That's ridiculous," she said. "Even if the chain was cut, it was probably done as a prank by some kid from town. They must hate us tourists for overrunning their village."

Nancy looked skeptical. "But tourists also provide jobs for their parents. I don't think they mind us that much."

"Look, I don't know why the sign fell," Rachel said earnestly. "But I'm sure it's nothing."

Nancy bit her lip. In her experience, people acted scared when they were told someone was out to hurt them. Why didn't Rachel care?

Nancy flashed the note she'd found. "I found this lying on the ground where you fell, Rachel."

Rachel glanced at the scrap of paper. Her face hardened. "Never saw it," she claimed. Yet Nancy thought she saw Rachel's pale skin flush beneath her freckles.

"Me neither," Rhonda spoke up, though Nancy hadn't asked her.

Just then, another knock came on the door. "Hello, it's Dr. Finney. Miss Selkirk?"

"You'd better go now, Nancy," Rhonda said firmly. "See you tomorrow." And Nancy had no choice but to walk out.

"I never eat this much for breakfast," Bess exclaimed, rising from the table. "Eggs, bacon, toast, *and* those yummy fried tomatoes."

"You were hungry, and no wonder; you spent all day yesterday exercising," George said. "Today will be more of the same. That's why I had two bowls of oatmeal—so I can keep up with Rhonda."

Nancy wrinkled her nose. "I'm not sure Rhonda will agree to ride with you today—or Rachel with me," she said. "Not after I spilled the beans to them last night. What was I thinking?"

"You were thinking they'd be glad to know you're a detective," Bess consoled her. "And anyone else would be. I think their reaction is highly suspicious."

Nancy smiled, grateful for her friend's loyal support. "Well, we should ride together today, and enjoy ourselves. I'll go find Bob and get our map and cell phone."

"Meet you by the bikes," Bess agreed.

Stepping outside, Nancy marveled at another

sunny day. "So much for all the Irish rain," she said to herself.

The tour group's bikes were lined up along a low stone wall, their chrome fittings glinting in the morning sun. None of the other cyclists were out yet. Nancy strolled to the corner of the hotel to check if Bob was anywhere nearby.

Rounding the corner of the white stucco inn, Nancy glanced down a narrow alley where a few cars were parked. Two people huddled together about fifty yards down the alley, in close conversation.

Nancy froze. It was Rhonda—whispering earnestly with the stranger in the black overcoat.

6

Look Both Ways

With long, determined strides, Nancy headed toward Rhonda and the mysterious man. Something's up with those two, she told herself, and I'm going to find out what it is.

But as soon as she began to approach, the man saw her from the corner of his eye and immediately started to back away from Rhonda. He raised his voice, and Nancy clearly heard him say, "Thank you, miss, I'll find it on me own."

I'll bet that was for my benefit, Nancy thought.

Moving with surprising agility for such a large person, the man whisked around a corner before Nancy reached Rhonda. The Australian girl turned to face Nancy, looking startled.

"Why, Nancy," she said, adjusting the zipper on

her neon green spandex jersey. "G'day. Ready for today's ride?"

Nancy refused to be distracted. "Who was that man you were just talking to? Everything okay?" she asked.

Rhonda pursed her lips. "What man?"

"The man in the black coat," Nancy said, her fists on her hips.

"How should I know?" Rhonda replied with an airy shrug. "He was just a tourist asking for directions. He took me for a local. Fancy that! I told him I was probably just as lost as he was."

"Lost?" Nancy narrowed her eyes. "This is a small village. How could anyone be lost here?"

"Well, he got mixed up—didn't know which pub was which, I reckon," Rhonda explained, waving her hand.

She turned on her heel and started to hurry away. Unfortunately for Rhonda, the cleats on her cycling shoes clattered and slid on the cobblestoned street. Nancy, wearing her low-tech cross-trainers, easily caught up as Rhonda headed for the main street.

"The funny thing is, I've seen that man before," she persisted, closely observing Rhonda's expression. "The day we landed at Shannon Airport. I remember noticing him because he's missing one finger."

"Is that so?" Rhonda's face was like a mask of total

unconcern. "I didn't get that close a look. You've got a knack for identifying people. Must be your "detective eyes.""

"Yes," Nancy said, ignoring the dig. "But don't you think it's strange he would show up here? That can't be another coincidence."

"Why not?" Rhonda said calmly, walking on up the street. "Ireland's an awfully small country, and this is one of its most popular tourist stops. I reckon half the people who came through Shannon the other day will be driving up and down this coast. It's no surprise you'd run into someone twice. I wouldn't worry about it. Now, excuse me, I've got to buy some film for my camera." She popped into a small shop that was open early, leaving Nancy alone on the cobbled pavement.

Frustrated, Nancy went back to where the bikes were parked beside the inn entrance. Bess and George were packing supplies for the day's ride in their canvas panniers—bags fitted onto a bracket mounted over the rear wheels.

"Bob gave us our map and cell phone," Bess told Nancy. "We can get going whenever you're ready. Maybe if we get a head start on the others, we won't have to ride so fast."

Nancy chewed her lip for a second. Her natural desire to help people was winning out over her stung sense of pride. "Slight change in plans," she announced. "I think we should do everything we can to follow the Selkirks again today."

Bess groaned and sagged against the stone wall. "Why?"

"You'll never guess who I just saw," Nancy explained quietly, hoping none of the other gathering tour members would overhear. "Remember that suspicious guy I noticed at the airport?"

Bess raised her eyebrows. "The one with the missing finger?"

"Yes," Nancy said. "And guess who was talking to him? Rhonda."

George whistled softly.

"She said he was just asking directions," Nancy added, "but the way they were talking sure looked like they knew each other well."

George glanced around to look for the Selkirks. "Once again, Rhonda pretends not to know something she obviously does know," she muttered.

Nancy nodded. "And it does seem significant that this guy's in town, doesn't it? Considering what happened to Rachel last night."

"But after that note you found, I thought it was Derek who lured Rachel outside," Bess said.

"Ooh, do I detect a change of heart?" George needled Bess. "You're not defending Derek anymore. Could it be because he spent all last night

54

flirting with both Rhonda and Rachel?"

Bess blushed slightly, but she held her ground. "Working with Nancy, I've learned one thing: Don't ignore the evidence."

Nancy pushed up the sleeves of her yellow windbreaker. "I wish we knew whether the note was for Rhonda or for Rachel."

"I had a thought in the middle of the night," George said. "Suppose Derek passed the note to Rhonda, and Rachel saw it. Maybe she went outside to stop Derek from having a private date with her sister."

"Or Rhonda went outside to stop Rachel from meeting Derek," Bess said. "The possibilities in this love triangle are endless."

At that moment, Derek and Camilla strolled out of the inn. As Camilla pulled on a pair of stretchy leather cycling gloves, Derek walked behind, his hands resting on her shoulders. Camilla halted for a moment and leaned back against his chest, smiling warmly up at him.

"They look lovey-dovey this morning," Nancy observed. "Isn't it weird that Camilla doesn't seem to mind Derek flirting with the Selkirks?" She fit her helmet over her hair. "This isn't just a love triangle, it's a love quadrangle. Something's definitely weird."

Now Rachel appeared at the inn doorway, pausing for a moment on the flagstone step to draw in a lungful of breezy sea air. She had a strip of gauze around her head, half covering her copper-colored hair, but she was decked out in full cycling gear, black and fluorescent orange. Nancy had to admire the Australian girl's spirit, even though she did question her judgment.

"Hey, Rachel, how's the head?" Natalie de Fusco called over in a friendly voice.

Rachel smiled shyly and touched her bandage. "I'm feeling super, really I am," she replied. "Takes more than a little knock on the head to put me out of action. The bandage is just so my helmet won't irritate the cut. But the doctor says I'm perfectly fit to ride."

Bob Prendergast turned around from where he was discussing the day's route with Carl Thompson. "I know the doctor gave you a clean bill of health, Rachel," he said, "but could you promise to take it easy today? Just so I don't have a heart attack?"

Rachel chuckled. "Anything for you, Bob."

"Then take the inland route instead of the coastal one," Bob advised, pointing to two different roads on the photocopied map. "It's five miles shorter and a lot less hilly. You're riding on a rocky plateau instead of up and down seaside bluffs. Besides, it's more interesting scenery."

"Whatever you say," Rachel agreed.

As Rachel strolled toward her bike, Nancy stepped forward. "Morning, Rachel," she said.

Rachel shot her a wary glance. "Morning, Nancy. Hi, George and Bess."

Inwardly, Nancy groaned. Telling the Selkirks that she was a detective hadn't helped her get close to them, as she had hoped. In fact, it had driven them away.

Luckily, George was thinking fast. "Looks like Rhonda's not here yet," she said brightly. "Want to ride together this morning, Rachel? That way, I can compare your speed with your sister's."

Evidently, George had pushed the right button. A competitive gleam lit up Rachel's face. "I did promise Bob I'd go easy," she said with a mischievous smile, "but a challenge is a challenge. Let's go!"

Nancy flashed a look of gratitude at her friend. With a wink, George took her ten-speed by the handlebars and walked it over to where Rachel was getting her magenta bike ready.

"What about Rhonda?" Bess asked Nancy, craning her neck to look around. "She still hasn't shown up. Are you going to try to ride with her?"

Nancy shook her head. "I don't think she'd let me, judging from how she talked to me this morning." She sighed. She suspected she would like Rachel and Rhonda if she ever got to know them better. Now, that didn't look likely.

"No," Nancy decided. "If we want to keep an eye on Rhonda, we'll just have to ride close behind her."

Bess made a face. "And here I was looking forward to a leisurely day of cycling. I guess this means we won't be able to take the shorter inland route."

"Sorry, pal," Nancy said, playfully bumping her friend's arm with her fist. "If Rhonda takes the coast road—and I bet she will—we've got to follow."

Across the paved area, Nancy saw Rachel swing her left leg over the crossbar of her bike. George thrust her feet in the toe clips on her pedals. "See you at lunch!" George called out with a wave to Nancy and Bess.

Bumping over the cobblestones, Rachel darted onto the main road, inserting herself into traffic right behind a small green car. George stood on her pedals, pumping to catch up.

George turned onto the road, eyes trained on Rachel, who was already picking up speed.

Suddenly, the tour's cherry red van roared out of the side alley. Terry O'Leary was at the wheel. He gunned the van, lurching onto the road—aiming for George!

7

A Vicious Cycle

Scared by the engine's roar behind her, George clutched her brakes and wrenched the bike aside.

Nancy dropped her bike and ran toward George. For a moment, Nancy lost sight of her friend as the van screeched between them.

Suddenly, Nancy heard a sickening thud.

The van jerked to a stop. Terry O'Leary threw open his door. "Eh, what is it now?" he grumbled.

Nancy ran around the corner of the van, Bess at her heels. George sat on the pavement, looking dazed.

"Now I know why cyclists wear helmets," George said, looking up at her friends. "I flew over the handlebars and landed on my head, but I'm actually fine."

Terry stood behind Nancy, awkwardly opening and closing his fists. "You want to watch where you're riding," he said to George. "You can't just go barging into oncoming traffic."

Bob came bustling around the van, looking agitated. "Terry, you idiot!" he lashed out at his driver. "How many times do I have to tell you?"

"Coming out of that alley, I couldn't see her," Terry protested, his pale gray eyes shifting nervously.

"Then that's when you should drive slowly," Bob said, sounding exasperated.

"But I had to accelerate to get up the incline. There were cars coming," Terry defended himself.

"Yeah, right—the dreaded rush hour traffic in Doolin," Bob muttered sarcastically. "Are you okay, George?"

"A little shaken, that's all," she said, standing up and brushing off her blue cycling shorts. "A scrape on my leg, maybe."

"She scratched the paint!" Terry complained, pointing to the side of the red van. "And after we just got a new paint job."

Bob groaned. "Terry, forget the paint! One of our guests got hurt—and it could have been a lot worse. Now shut up and get me the first-aid kit."

Terry flashed a dark look at Bob and hurried to the passenger door. He handed Nancy a flat metal box with a Red Cross on its lid. Inside, Nancy found some alcohol and a cotton pad. She began to swab George's scraped knee clean.

"Where's Rachel?" George asked.

"She went on riding—she didn't even see your collision," Bess reported. "Rhonda showed up and went to catch up with Rachel."

"So much for riding with them," George said with a sigh.

"It doesn't matter," Nancy said, repacking the first-aid kit. She glanced over at Terry and Bob standing a short distance away. Bob was talking angrily; Terry hung his head and listened with a smoldering look on his face.

"I wouldn't be in Terry's shoes now for anything," Bess said sympathetically.

Nancy crooked an eyebrow. "Maybe. But it looks like Bob has read him the riot act plenty of times before. There's some bad history between them. Wish I knew what it was."

Bess followed Nancy's gaze. "You don't think Terry's up to something, do you?"

Nancy considered. "Well, it was Terry who spilled that suspicious soda two nights ago—and last night he was close by when the sign fell on Rachel."

George shivered. "You don't think Terry was *trying* to hit me just now, do you?"

"It happened so fast, I'm not sure what I saw," Nancy admitted. "But something about this guy doesn't add up."

Knowing that George wasn't really hurt, the rest

of the group soon mounted their bikes and set off. Nancy, Bess, and George followed. The three girls soon passed the de Fuscos, then Derek and Camilla, who were dawdling along.

Before long, they reached a fork. "We got a late start—might as well take the shortcut," Nancy said, turning onto the road heading inland.

"Yes!" Bess pumped her arm.

"Rhonda and Rachel probably followed the coast road," George guessed.

"Don't bet on it," Nancy said, peering along the road ahead. "I see two tiny figures way ahead. They're far away, but one of them is bright green and the other one orange. And if I remember correctly—"

"Rachel was definitely wearing orange this morning," Bess said. "And Rhonda was in green."

Nancy grinned. "Ready to kick it up a notch?"

Bess groaned, but Nancy and George began to pedal hard, and she had no choice but to keep up.

"They're leading a stiff pace," Nancy called out. "So much for Rachel taking it easy."

"It's a good thing they didn't notice we're behind them," George shouted.

"Yeah—I'd hate to see how hard they'd ride if they were *trying* to go fast," panted Bess.

"Hey, they just pulled over to the side of the road," George said. "Now we can catch up."

"Why did they stop?" Nancy wondered aloud.

"Looks like they're checking out that herd of sheep," George guessed.

"*Flock* of sheep," Bess corrected her cousin, leaning over her handlebars. "Cows go in herds, sheep are in flocks. Aren't they fluffy and adorable? I can't wait to see them up close."

"Uh-oh." Nancy began to reach for her hand brakes. "We may be more up close than we want."

The gray asphalt ahead was slowly covered by white as the immense flock of sheep began to wander onto the road. A chorus of *baa*s rose on the air, echoing off the grassy hollows.

"Slow down—they're blocking the road!" George called out.

As Nancy pressed her hand brakes, she gazed past the sheep. Rhonda and Rachel had hopped back onto their bikes and were pedaling away. Rachel waved jauntily over her head at Nancy and her friends, stranded amidst the woolly flood.

"Do you think they did that on purpose?" Nancy asked as she stopped, helpless, surrounded by sheep.

The animals' fat sides heaved under thick, ivory-colored fleeces. Tiny black hooves clicked aimlessly on the pavement. "I didn't realize how many there were," Bess said, glancing skittishly from side to side. "This is creepy. How long do you think it'll take them to cross the road?"

"They aren't exactly crossing," George said, frowning. "There's no dog or shepherd guiding them. They're just crashing around like bumper cars."

"I bet Rhonda and Rachel opened that gate," Nancy said, pointing to a swinging wicket at the edge of the nearby pasture. "They lured them onto the road to stop us!"

Looking back up the road, Nancy saw a pair of cyclists approach. It was Derek and Camilla. Nancy grimaced, embarrassed.

As the English pair coasted up, Bess waved to them. "Looks like Rhonda and Rachel let these sheep out," she called out, "and now we're stuck."

"Trust a pair of Australians to know about sheep," Derek said with an amused smirk. "But don't worry, we'll help you herd them back."

It took some doing, but fifteen minutes later they had steered the sheep back into the pasture. Derek fastened the gate shut. "The Selkirks got you this time," he teased.

Nancy gave a rueful shrug. "Let's just head on to lunch."

At the crest of the next steep hill, they looked down the hillside, expecting to see the vivid green expanses they had become used to. George braked to a stop. "Wow! What happened?"

The others braked, too. Below them stretched a vast panorama of creased, craggy gray rock. Bess shivered. "I feel like we just took a wrong turn and ended up on the moon."

"Amazing," Nancy exclaimed. "I've never seen a landscape quite like this."

"This must be what they call the Burren," Derek read from the map.

George pointed downhill. "Look, there's Carl. Let's catch up to him."

"You go on—I want to snap some photos," Derek said, pulling his camera out of its case.

As Nancy and her friends waved good-bye and pedaled on, something struck Nancy. *Odd,* she thought. *A panoramic lens would be the thing to catch this wide landscape. So why does Derek have that huge telephoto lens on his camera? That's like what cops use on a stakeout.*

Carl Thompson had parked his bike by the side of the road and was kneeling on the gray rock. "We didn't see you pass us earlier," Bess remarked as they reached the professor.

Carl looked up and grinned. "I didn't. I left early, while you all were still at breakfast. I wanted to give myself plenty of time to explore the Burren—it's the main thing I came here to see. As a geologist, I find it fascinating."

"Geologist? I thought you were a chemist," Bess said.

Carl smiled modestly. "Double specialty."

"Well, I find it fascinating, too, and I'm neither a geologist nor a chemist," said Nancy.

"What kind of rock is it?" George asked.

"Limestone, mostly," Carl said. "This kind of region is called 'karst.' You see how it has heaved around over the centuries? That's what caused all these cracks and fissures in the surface—or, as the locals call it, the 'pavements.' Now, look inside the fissures. You'll find a whole secret world."

The girls dismounted, and bess poked a finger into one crevice. "You'd almost expect tiny people to be living there."

George punched her cousin's shoulder. "No leprechaun sightings, Bess, please!"

"It's a beautiful place," Nancy said, sitting on her heels and gazing around in awe. "So primitive-looking."

Carl nodded. "The Selkirks said it reminded them of the Outback. Except, of course, that the rock there is red sandstone, not gray limestone."

Nancy raised her eyebrows. "The Selkirks? When did they come by?"

"About ten minutes ago," Carl said. "They stopped to look at it with me, too."

Nancy got up, peering along the road ahead.

There was no sign of the sisters, but they could be hidden in a road dip. "Well, thanks so much for the info," she said. "We'd better get moving."

"See you at lunch. We're stopping at the Cave of Ailwee," Carl said. "Carved by an underground river out of limestone. Fascinating!"

Bess and George remounted their bikes, too, saying good-bye to the professor. They hadn't gone far before George said, "There they are!"

Two tiny figures—one in neon green, the other in fluorescent orange—were outlined against the horizon, scooting briskly along. Sunlight glinted off their magenta bikes.

Bess moaned. "They're so far ahead, how can we possibly catch up?"

"They probably think we're still back with the sheep," Nancy reasoned. "That'll buy us some time." She stood up on her pedals and began to pump hard.

From the top of the plateau, Nancy saw the scene unfold like an old silent movie. As the Selkirks coasted down a long hill, a blue car turned onto the road. As soon as the sisters passed it, it began to pick up speed.

Nancy tensed up, clutching her handlebars. How ever fast the Selkirks might be riding, the blue car was going faster.

The Australians shifted toward the left, giving the

car room to pass. But instead of swerving around them, the car kept bearing down toward them. Rachel glanced over her shoulder, balancing on the rim of the asphalt.

Bess let out an anguished cry. "The car's going to run them off the road!"

8

The Chase Is On

The blue car surged toward the Selkirk girls. The screech of its tires ominously carried across the high, still air to Nancy, Bess, and George.

As if in slow motion, Nancy saw the car ram the rear wheel of Rachel's bike. Nancy squinted to try to see a bit better. Rachel, looking like a mere flicker of orange, flipped off the road and into a ditch.

Twisting around in her seat, Rhonda let out a scream, tiny and futile-sounding at this distance. She bailed out, leaping off her bike just before the car reached her. She tumbled into the same ditch where Rachel had landed.

The blue car, without a pause, revved up and sped away.

"Come on—we've got to go help!" Nancy cried.

The three River Heights girls began to race their bikes down the long, winding road. "Did you get a good look at the car?" George asked Nancy as they rode abreast.

Nancy shook her head. "Too far off—no way I could get a license number. I couldn't even identify the make. I don't know European models as well as I do American ones."

Dropping into a dip in the road, the girls briefly lost sight of the Selkirks, but when they came out again they saw Rhonda and Rachel climbing out of the ditch, brushing themselves off. "They don't look badly hurt," Bess shouted, relieved.

Just then, Nancy heard another car engine roar behind them. She swerved sharply behind George to let it pass, almost crashing into Bess.

Looking over her shoulder, Nancy saw it was the red McElheney Tours van. Terry O'Leary was bent over the steering wheel, jaw jutting forward, glaring at the highway. He beeped the horn and raced by, evidently headed for Rachel and Rhonda.

"That was convenient, wasn't it?" George said, slackening her pace.

"Too convenient," Nancy replied. "How did he know they'd had an accident? Let's hurry."

"Why?" Bess pleaded. "Now that help has arrived—"

"How do we know Terry will help?" Nancy answered. "He almost hit George this morning, remember? I don't want to leave him alone with Rhonda and Rachel."

Nancy whizzed down the hill, soon pulling up to the accident site. Rhonda and Rachel sat slumped by the roadside, near where Terry had parked the van. Terry was hiking up out of the steep ditch, holding aloft a magenta bike. "This one's got a bent wheel," he announced. "I'll have to go into Galway to get it replaced. You can ride along in the van—but you'll have to skip the cave." He blinked, his eyes sliding from one of the sisters to the other. "Which one of you belongs to this bike?"

Rhonda and Rachel traded glances. "It's mine," Rhonda said, climbing to her feet. She winced as she tried to rotate her shoulder. "I don't mind missing the cave. I feel a little banged up, anyway—must have landed funny."

Rachel looked past Terry. "Hello, Nancy," she greeted her. "Glad to see you. Thanks for phoning Terry to come help us."

"I didn't phone Terry," Nancy said, feeling guilty that the idea hadn't occurred to her.

They heard a whirr of wheels behind them. "It wasn't her—it was me," Carl Thompson announced, pulling up. "Derek and Camilla and I saw you from up the hill."

Nancy twisted around and looked up the hill.

71

Derek and Camilla sat on their bikes at the summit—and Derek was peering through his telephoto lens. Nancy winced, remembering Derek pointing his camera at Rhonda after she passed out that first night. Did the guy have no sense of shame?

"Well, thanks a million, Carl," Rachel said.

Terry carried the bike with the bent wheel to the van. As the sun shone on its handlebars, Nancy noticed they were covered in silver tape. *Funny*, she mused. *I thought it was Rachel who put silver tape on her handlebars, not Rhonda.*

"Should one of us go along with you?" Nancy offered. The idea of leaving Rhonda alone with Terry worried her.

Nancy thought she saw Rhonda stiffen. But before she could say anything, Terry whirled around, glaring at her. "No!" he barked. "No room. I've got the whole lot of luggage back there, and all the lunch as well. I barely have room for one bike and a passenger."

Rachel stood up, flexing a bruised leg. "I'm happy to ride on to the cave—it's not too much farther. I hear it's a beaut, with an underground waterfall and all."

"I'll get a doctor to look at your sister," Terry grumbled. He slammed the van's back door and stomped to the driver's side.

"Enjoy the cave, Rache," Rhonda said to her sister

with a wink as she climbed into the van.

"Feel better," Rachel replied.

Nancy anxiously watched the van pull away, hoping that Rhonda would be safe.

The van left, and the five cyclists—Nancy, Bess, George, Rachel, and Carl—got back onto their bikes.

"I owe you girls an apology," Rachel said as they reached cruising speed. "That was a sneaky trick Rhonda and I played on you with the sheep."

"What trick?" Carl asked.

Bess rolled her eyes. "We got stuck in the middle of a flock of sheep crossing the road."

Carl chuckled. "That must have been an experience."

"It was," Nancy agreed. "Well, I appreciate the apology, Rachel."

"Rhonda and I saw them milling around by the gate and couldn't resist," Rachel confessed. "Especially since you three seemed so keen to catch up with us. It was just a prank."

"Unfortunately, that incident with the car wasn't just a prank," Nancy said, still concerned about Rhonda's departure. "We saw it all from a distance. Did you recognize the car?"

"Recognize it?" Rachel looked puzzled. "No way. I don't know anybody in Ireland. Anyway, I never got a good look at the car. It was behind me the whole time."

"You know, it looked like the car hit your bike,"

Nancy said. "Rhonda only jumped off hers. Yet her wheel was bent, not yours. Isn't that strange?"

Rachel bit her lip. "Well, actually, it was my bike that got hurt. Rhonda said it was hers because she knew I wanted to go see the cave."

Nancy nodded. That explained the silver handlebar tape. But she wondered grimly if Rhonda had bought more trouble than she knew.

One thing Nancy had to say: The car accident had changed Rachel's attitude. She no longer seemed intent on ditching Nancy. They hung out together for the next couple of hours, enjoying their picnic lunch and then exploring the Cave of Ailwee. Though the underground cavern was illuminated, there were plenty of shadowy corners and eerie echoes. At one point, a simple drip of water off a stalactite made Rachel jump, and her foot slipped on the clammy cavern floor. Nancy grabbed her elbow just in time. Rachel flashed her a smile of gratitude.

Maybe Rachel has realized it's good to be with a detective, Nancy thought to herself. *Especially when so many dangerous things have happened— coincidence, or not.*

When they emerged from the cavern, blinking in the afternoon sunlight, Terry was waiting in the parking lot with the red van. He had already collected the bikes and had returned to drive the cyclists to Galway City. "There's not enough seats for everybody to ride at once. We'll have to make two trips," Bob explained.

"I'll go on the second shift," Derek volunteered. "Rachel, why don't you wait with me?"

Nancy noticed Camilla, standing behind Derek, give him a little jab in the ribs. *Good for you*, Nancy thought.

Rachel hesitated. "Actually, Derek, I'd like to get to Galway and make sure Rhonda's okay."

"I saw her at the hotel; everything's fine," Bob assured Rachel. "She had a soak in a hot bath and she's feeling one hundred percent."

Nancy blew a tiny sigh of relief.

"I could use a hot bath," Natalie de Fusco put in. "I call first shift."

Nancy, Bess, and George agreed to ride with Derek and Camilla on the second trip. After the first group had driven away, Derek and Camilla strolled around the grounds. "Look—Camilla's giving Derek a piece of her mind," George noted dryly, nodding to where the English pair were having a heated conversation.

"It's about time," Bess said. "Even I'm tired of the way he throws himself at the Selkirks."

"Jealous?" George asked.

"Not anymore," Bess said. "He may be totally hot-looking, but who'd want a boyfriend who flirts with other girls?"

"Do you still think he's behind all these accidents?" George asked Nancy.

Nancy cupped her chin in her hand. "I don't know. He couldn't have been driving that blue car. He was riding right behind us."

"It wasn't Terry O'Leary, either—he showed up in the van soon after," Bess pointed out.

Nancy nodded. "But Terry could be working with the driver of the blue car," she suggested. "We know he was somewhere nearby, since he arrived so fast. And he sure was eager to take Rhonda away in the van. Thank goodness she got back okay."

"One thing occurs to me," George said. "What if all these incidents are aimed at McElheney Tours itself? It could be sabotage from a rival company. That falling sign and the poisoned soda might have been aimed at anybody. And it was me who got hit by the van this morning."

"Yes, but you were right behind Rachel," Bess pointed out. "It could have hit you by mistake."

"Well, it is a theory," Nancy said. "But three out of four incidents so far have involved the Selkirk sisters. I'm afraid we'll have to see what happens next, if anything."

Terry and Bob soon returned, and the five remaining tour members piled into the red van. The drive around the bay didn't take long. Soon they were sweeping down into Galway City. The girls sat up eagerly, looking out the van windows.

Bob slid forward on his seat to deliver his usual travelogue. "Lots of people think Galway City is Ireland's prettiest city," he said. "The downtown area is remarkably well-preserved and quaint, but there's a university here and lots of arts and culture. In its heyday as a port, Galway had a thriving trade with Spain—it's said that Christopher Columbus made his last stop here on his way to America. In the sixteenth century . . ."

Nancy leaned back and let Bob's words wash over her. It would be nice to be in a city again for a night, she decided. She enjoyed riding from village to village, but her legs weren't used to so much exercise—especially not at the speeds she had to ride to keep up with the Selkirks.

Nancy must have dropped off, because the next thing she knew, George was shaking her awake. "Nancy, we're here. Bess is going up to the room. I want to check out this cool pottery store I noticed as we were riding into town."

Nancy shook herself. "Pottery? I'm up for that." She climbed out of the van and followed George down the sidewalk from the hotel.

The girls plunged into the narrow medieval streets of downtown Galway City. Like a maze, the streets twisted and wound between overhanging old buildings. "This is so cool!" Nancy exclaimed.

"Here's the shop," George announced. She marched into a quaint-looking shop front with tiny windows. Inside, however, was a well-lit, modern store, its open display shelves lined with beautiful hand-thrown pieces of glazed ceramics by local artists.

Browsing among the shelves, Nancy reached out to touch one bowl. It would make a perfect gift for Hannah Gruen, the housekeeper who had cared for Nancy ever since Nancy's mother died. Nancy lifted the bowl gently, admiring its smooth, greenish glaze and sinuous curves.

A man's hand was reaching into the case from the other side to grasp a mug. His coat sleeve was heavy black wool—and the little finger was missing from his left hand!

9

Slipping Away

Holding her breath, Nancy sidled around the floor-to-ceiling display case. Was it the same man she'd seen at Shannon? The same man who'd been talking to Rhonda in the alley that morning?

Peeking around the corner of the display case, Nancy got her first really good look at the mystery man. His broad shoulders, massive forehead, and terse expression were what had drawn her attention before. Now she took in his short, greasy brown hair and small, dark eyes. He looked like he was in his mid-thirties. Beneath the formal-looking overcoat, he wore faded jeans and sneakers.

As the man looked over his shoulder, Nancy ducked so he wouldn't see her. "Miss?" she heard his harsh, nasal voice call out to the shopkeeper.

"Yes?" The shopkeeper strolled over to him.

"The sign says this pattern is called Clostermeade Manor," the man said. His accent certainly sounded Australian, Nancy thought.

"Yes, that's what the potter named it."

"I had an aunt who was parlor maid at Clostermeade Manor before she came out to Australia," the man said. "She always showed me pictures of the place. Tell me, would Clostermeade be near here?"

Leaning forward to listen, Nancy brushed accidentally against a display shelf. The ceramic pieces on the shelf wobbled and clinked.

She could hear the man hastily plunk down the mug and brush past the sales clerk. Nancy whirled around and pretended to browse on another shelf. *Please don't recognize me*, she wished silently.

Then she heard a heavy tread and the shop door swishing open. Nancy sprang to where she could see the doorway. A broad-shouldered back, clad in black wool, was shoving hurriedly out to the street.

"George, come on!" Nancy called her friend.

George, well-used to Nancy's sudden moves, set down the casserole dish she'd been admiring. "I'll be back," she promised the shopkeeper as she bounded across the store, following Nancy out to the street.

Nancy hesitated a moment on the sidewalk. "The way his body tilted, I'd guess he went to the right," she decided, and sprinted down the sloping street in that direction.

George was right behind her. "Who was it, Nan?"

"The Australian guy with the missing pinkie!"

Nancy felt pretty sure she'd seen a black shape turn left by the red-painted shop front across the way. Dodging and weaving through the afternoon shopping crowd, she raced around the corner after him.

Her quick eyes picked him out up ahead, this time popping into an alley to his right. Nimbly, Nancy leaped over a woman's shopping bag set down on the cobbles, and ducked under a display of finely woven shawls. She couldn't lose the trail this time!

Running into the mouth of the alley, Nancy spied the black coat up ahead. The man was running hard now—obviously he knew Nancy was after him. She urged her legs to go faster, willing herself to ignore the sore muscles of two days' bicycling.

The man swung left into a larger street. I'm closing in on him now, Nancy thought triumphantly. But as she turned left at the corner, she skidded to a halt. He was nowhere to be seen.

Nancy pivoted to the right, wondering if he'd faked her out with a false turn. She couldn't see him there, either.

Maybe he went into a store, she mused. But which? She peered into the large front window of a jewelry shop, but he wasn't there. She slipped into a bookstore across the street, searching between its rows of bookcases. No luck.

Nancy's throat tightened. The trail was swiftly growing cold. In the heart of a city, there were so many places where a man could hide.

Discouraged, she retraced her route through the winding narrow streets. She spotted George leaning against a brick wall. "Nancy, I lost you. Where'd you go?"

"He got away." Nancy sighed.

"Well, cheer up," George said. "When I couldn't find you, I circled around this block, and guess what?"

Nancy said eagerly, "You saw him?"

"No, but I saw his car." George's eyes gleamed. "Or rather, I saw the blue car. But all the evidence suggests it's his, doesn't it?"

Nancy drew a careful breath. "We can't assume anything. But let's go have a look."

George led Nancy around a couple of corners and emerged in front of a beautiful little gray stone church, crammed between two larger buildings. There was an empty space at the curb by the wrought-iron church gate.

George's face crumpled in disappointment. "It was right there! A blue four-door sedan—same size, same color, same style as the one that chased Rhonda and Rachel today."

Nancy swallowed her hope. "Don't fret, George. We have no proof it belongs to our Mr. Black, anyway."

"But if we could have seen who got into it . . ." George slammed her fist into her palm in frustration.

"He may have run back to get the car as soon as he shook me off his trail," Nancy said. "If so, we have no hope of catching him on foot."

"Well, at least I wrote down the license plate number," George said.

Nancy clapped her friend on the shoulder. "Good work, George!"

"Hey, I haven't tagged along on all your cases for nothing," George remarked. She bent over and fished a folded scrap of paper out of her shoe. "One bad thing about these cycling shorts: no pockets," she noted with a rueful grin.

Nancy studied the paper, a torn-off bit of newspaper. "G500A7," she read.

"Are you going to ask the police to check it out?"

Nancy scrunched up her nose. "Frankly, George, I don't think they'd cooperate. This isn't River Heights, where the police might check a license number for me because they know me and my dad. The Irish police—or the Garda, as they're called—have no reason to take my word I'm a detective. And there's no actual crime to investigate. Rhonda and Rachel haven't reported anything to the authorities, remember."

"What if we got Bob to report the incidents?"

George suggested. "His company does a lot of business in Ireland. Considering how important tourism is around here, I'd think the police would be anxious to protect innocent travelers."

Nancy cocked her head. "It's worth a try. My sense is that Bob is getting worried about all these accidents. And if he isn't, he should be."

Nancy looked discouraged when she joined Bess and George in their hotel room a couple of hours later. "What did Bob say?" George asked.

Nancy plopped down on the bed with its sprigged muslin counterpane. Tonight's lodging was a charming bed-and-breakfast, full of antiques. "Bob says he can't go to the police without Rhonda's and Rachel's permission," Nancy reported. "He was adamant about it."

"Why are they so reluctant to take any help?" Bess wondered, turning from the mirror where she'd been admiring her pale blue sweater.

Nancy shrugged. "I don't know, but Bob's so afraid of crossing them, he can hardly think straight. He kept saying this is just a string of ordinary mishaps—but from the tone of his voice, I don't think he believes that himself."

Wearily she opened her suitcase, pulling out the navy knit dress she planned to wear to dinner. The tour group was eating tonight at a seafood restaurant on Quay Street, near the Galway harbor.

"I suspect Rhonda and Rachel aren't just any customers," George said. "They certainly seem rich, for one thing."

"I agree," Nancy said. "All the more reason why someone might really be after them."

"Like our Mr. Black?" Bess asked.

"Or Terry O'Leary, or Derek—or whoever was driving that blue car," Nancy said, pondering as she unbuttoned her shirt. "We've got an open field of suspects. One thing I do know: Mr. Black knows I'm on his trail, and he sure acts like he's got something to hide."

"So this is officially a case, Nancy?" George asked.

Nancy blew out a sigh. "If it is, it's a weird sort of case. I don't really have a client—Rhonda and Rachel never hired me."

"In fact, they keep avoiding you," George said.

"That's not true. Rachel's friendly again," Bess remarked.

"Yes, but that was today, when Rachel was on her own. With Rhonda back on the scene, I bet things will be different," Nancy warned.

"Gathering evidence will be tough," George said. "We're constantly on the move; not only the suspects, but the victims as well."

"And we ourselves have to keep moving," Nancy added. "We can't go back and forth investigating the scenes of these crimes."

"Especially not when we're only on bikes," Bess said.

"All the same, I've got to do something. I can't just sit around." And Nancy pressed her lips together in a determined expression her friends knew very well.

Nancy made a point of lingering the next morning over her breakfast of soda bread and grilled fish. She watched as the other members of the tour went off to start their rides: first Rachel and Rhonda; then the de Fuscos and Carl Thompson; and finally, Derek and Camilla with Bob. Bess and George were the last to get on their bikes. "Bob thinks I'm riding with you guys," Nancy reminded them as they stood in front of the hotel. "So don't ride too fast, and I'll catch up as soon as I'm done."

"Keep an eye out for Terry," George reminded her. "The van's still in the parking lot, waiting for him to load the luggage."

"I'll be careful," Nancy promised. She waved to her friends as they wheeled into the quiet street outside the bed-and-breakfast.

As soon as the coast seemed clear, Nancy walked back into the bed-and-breakfast. Looking as nonchalant as possible, she went up the mahogany staircase to the second floor. She sauntered down the wide, sunny hallway to room number four, the room where Rachel and Rhonda had slept last night.

A red-haired teenager was bustling down the hall with an armload of dirty sheets. "Oh, miss?" Nancy said. "I just checked out of room four, and I'm missing something. Could you open the door so I can check if I left it in my room?"

The maid shrugged. "No bother, ma'am." She dropped the linens in a heap and pulled a master key from her apron pocket. In a minute, Nancy was in Rhonda and Rachel's room.

She was taken aback to see how messy the girls had left the room. *They must be used to having servants pick up for them*, she thought. Sheets were half pulled off the bed, and wet towels lay in puddles on the carpet. Balled-up candy wrappers were strewn over the desk. A half-empty bottle of nail polish stood on the TV set, brush balanced precariously on top. Empty soda cans were lined up on the antique dresser, leaving white rings on its dark polished top.

Keeping an eye on the half-open door, Nancy began to methodically inspect the room. She started with the wastebasket, but it was empty. Beside it, however, lay a crumpled copy of a tabloid newspaper. She scooped its pages into order and stuffed it in her small daypack to read later. Who knew—it might contain a clue.

Just then, the door was thrust open. Nancy straightened up with a jerk and whirled around.

There stood Derek Thorogood, looking as shocked to see her as she was to see him.

"Derek—what are you doing here?" Nancy gasped.

Derek glared. "First you'd better tell me what *you're* doing here, Nancy."

10

Who's After Whom?

Nancy knew she had to act cool. "I'm doing Rhonda a favor. She asked me to come back and grab her guidebook." She dug her hand into her daypack and pulled out her own travel guide to Ireland. "See? Here it is."

Derek tilted his head in a way that told Nancy he wasn't convinced. "Well, I came back to get a cable for my laptop. Silly me—I left it in the outlet."

"In Rhonda and Rachel's room?" Nancy cast him a suspicious look. What was Derek up to?

Derek raised his eyebrows, looking innocent. "This is their room?"

"Unless you wear nail polish, it is," Nancy said, pointing to the bottle on the TV set.

"Oh, I never wear nail polish;—at least not in the daytime," Derek joked. He flashed Nancy a charming smile—one he used to get out of jams, Nancy suspected. "But you're right—now I realize this wasn't my room. I get so confused, staying in a new hotel every night."

It struck Nancy that Derek might have come back here for the same reason she had: to search Rhonda and Rachel's room. But why? What could he be hunting for?

"You'd better go look for your own room," Nancy said. "Good luck finding your cable."

"Now that you've fetched Rhonda's book," Derek said, nodding toward the guidebook in her hand, "you can accompany me."

Nancy stifled a groan. She'd never be able to search the room with Derek hovering around, and he seemed to know it.

Their eyes locked, each one determined not to leave the other in the room. The standoff ended only when the maid peeked around the door. "Did you find what you left, miss?"

Nancy gave a sigh of surrender. "Yes, thank you." She trudged out of the room, Derek following her. The maid pulled the door shut behind them. Nancy heard the lock click.

"So which room was yours?" Nancy said, trying to pin Derek down.

"Other end of the hall, I think," Derek said. He strolled to an open door with a brass numeral 8 on it. "This was it. I remember now."

He stuck his head briefly inside the room. "Not here. Perhaps I unplugged the cable after all, and packed it in the side pocket of my case. I'll check tonight. Not to worry—if I've lost it, it's easily replaced. Well, Nancy"—he gestured toward the staircase—"shall we go?"

Nancy strode down the hallway and downstairs, fighting to hide her irritation. *Only a temporary setback*, she told herself. *Tonight I'll find a way to search Rhonda and Rachel's bedroom, wherever we're staying. That'll be better, anyway, while their stuff's actually in the room.*

Walking outside, Nancy saw Derek's ten-speed propped against the garden fence beside hers. "At least now we can ride together," Nancy said.

"Super. I've got one of the mobiles," Derek said, showing her the cell phone, "and a copy of today's map."

Just then, the red tour van came rumbling out of the parking lot. Terry O'Leary braked when he saw them and rolled down his window. "No lagging about," he said crossly. "You'll be missing the ferry. There's not another for hours."

"We'll hurry," Nancy promised.

Luckily, their ride was all downhill from the B&B

to the harbor. A steam ferryboat was waiting at the docks, its engine rumbling. As soon as Nancy and Derek rode up the gangplank, the crew raised it and the boat set off. "Whew, that was tight," Derek said lightly. "Shall we find the others?"

George and Bess looked relieved when Nancy arrived on deck. "Glad you made it," George said. "Find anything?"

"Just Derek," Nancy murmured. Bess and George raised their eyebrows. But Derek was moving toward them, and she couldn't say more.

The ocean air was salty and brisk, and Nancy tugged her baseball cap tighter over her red-blond hair. Derek leaned suavely on the railing next to Bess and launched into a stream of chatter, but Nancy tuned it out.

She reviewed in her mind the facts of the case. The Australian man—or Mr. Black, as Nancy had nicknamed him—was her biggest question mark. But she still wanted to know more about Terry O'Leary. And Derek's appearance at the Selkirks' room this morning troubled her. What reason could he have for snooping in their room? *He's probably wondering the same thing about me,* Nancy told herself. That must be why he was sticking so close to her now, she realized with a flash of irritation.

As the ferry steamed across the harbor, the quaint medieval buildings of Galway City grew smaller and smaller, and the dark humps of land lying out in the ocean grew larger.

"If you thought County Clare was picturesque, wait till you see the Aran Isles," Bob said, joining them. "The smaller islands don't have car traffic, and some cottages still lack electricity or plumbing. The land is nearly as rocky as the Burren. Farmers have to make soil from sand and rotten seaweed."

Bess wrinkled her nose. "Ewww!"

Bob grinned. "I agree. If I lived here, I'd sure try to be a fisherman instead. But Aran Islanders are hardy, plain-living folks, used to fighting the elements."

"Most of them speak Gaelic, don't they?" Derek asked. "You know, the old Irish language."

Bob nodded. "Older folks do, and kids learn it in school. They're trying to keep it alive. But the same is true all over western Galway and Donegal. Look at the road signs; town names are usually in Gaelic as well as in English."

"How soon do we reach the island?" Bess asked.

"The ride over is three hours," Bob said. "Coming back, we can sail to Rossaveal, which only takes an hour. Too bad we only have time to see the big island, Inishmore. But the fort there, Dún Aengus, is spectacular. It's centuries old, and no one knows who built it, or why they needed to protect that lonesome bit of island. It's a mysterious ancient place, like Stonehenge."

Inishmore's port village, Kilronan, was a bit

touristy, with tour guides in minibuses buzzing around trying to pick up customers. Nancy was glad they had their bikes and could ride out of town on their own. The road to the ruined stone fort led straight out of Kilronan.

In only a few minutes the group was pedaling along a seaside line of cliffs. As usual, Rhonda and Rachel zipped off in front. But as Nancy and George began to follow, Derek pumped up behind them. "Can I ride with you two?"

"Sure," Nancy said, hiding her frustration.

From the looks of Derek's specialized cycling clothes and equipment, Nancy had assumed he was an expert cyclist. Now she learned differently. Derek had to look down at his gear levers every time he needed to shift. And despite his trim, athletic build, his legs weren't very muscular. As soon as he had to pedal hard, he lurched from side to side to give his legs an extra boost. George shot Nancy a meaningful glance behind Derek's back. She'd taught Nancy that extra motion like that dragged on the bike and slowed you down.

By the time the three of them reached the hilltop fort, the Selkirks' magenta bikes were already in the parking lot, along with Bob's silver racer. The McElheney van was parked there, too. Terry O'Leary sat in the driver's seat, eyes closed, snoring. "I guess he's seen this sight before," George remarked wryly as they parked their bikes.

Tourists swarmed over the broken stone ruins, perched at the edge of the cliff. Walking up a rocky rise to overlook the site, Nancy was impressed by how large the prehistoric fort was. It had been built in three concentric circles, the highest in the middle. Shallow depressions in the sparse grass showed where missing parts of the once-grand design had lain. The remaining stones, bleached pale by years of sea wind, reflected the sunshine with a hard glitter.

Nancy laid a hand on a nearby rock, awed by the thought of how long the rock had lain there. The stern gray stone was softened by patches of velvety moss and greenish gray lichens, flourishing in the wet sea air.

"Now there's a sight for you," Derek said, coming up behind her. With a sweep of his arm, he indicated the vast panorama of the flinty island and the mainland across the water. "That's a splendid view of Connemara over there."

Bess, cheeks still flushed from cycling, popped up behind Derek. "Connemara?" she said. "But we're looking east. Isn't that Galway?"

"The western part of Galway is also called Connemara," Derek said, pulling Bob's write-up out of the back pocket of his red spandex jersey.

With a glance Nancy signaled Bess to keep Derek occupied. Bess nodded. "But Carl was just telling me it was called the Gaeltacht," she said innocently, "because so many people there speak Gaelic. . . ." Nancy quietly backed away and left them.

She strode deeper into the fort, searching for the Selkirks. She soon spotted Rhonda, lounging on a large flat stone. Rhonda waved at Nancy. Nancy waved back, but a chill ran up her spine. It seemed disrespectful to her to climb onto these rocks that had endured so long, silent witnesses to the passing ages.

Still, since Rhonda was alone, it was an ideal time to question her. "We missed you at dinner last night," Nancy said, strolling over to her.

"I needed a night's rest," Rhonda said, propping herself on her elbows. "After my spill yesterday."

"Terry got your wheel fixed?"

"Oh, sure, good as new," Rhonda replied. No mention of the fact that it had been her sister's bike that had really needed the repair, Nancy noted.

"Any idea who hit you?"

Rhonda shrugged, her gaze sliding sideways. "Simple traffic thing, I reckon. Cyclists have them all the time."

"But after the trouble with the soda the first night . . . and your sister and the pub sign. . . ?"

Rhonda sat up and swung her legs over the side of the rock. She shot a piercing look at Nancy. "Look here, Nancy, what're you getting at?"

Nancy steeled herself. "I think someone's after you,"

she said. "The Australian man you were talking to yesterday morning—I saw him at Shannon, and I saw him again yesterday in Galway City. He's following us."

"I don't know any such bloke," Rhonda insisted. "Is this how you get all your cases, Nancy? By making things up? Well, excuse me, but I rode hard this morning. I'm ready to eat." She shouldered past Nancy and went toward Bob and Terry, who were laying out the picnic.

I blew it again, Nancy thought bitterly.

Reluctant to join the picnic just yet, Nancy looked around for Rachel. She spied her on the far side of the site, leaning dreamily on a shattered wall at the edge of the cliff.

Then Nancy saw Derek, hiding behind a nearby boulder, watching Rachel.

Quickly Nancy circled around the site, stumbling slightly in the overgrown ruts and declivities. Eyes on Rachel, she paused next to a taller fragment of wall. Her hand reached out to steady herself on its time-worn, pitted surface. She could see Rachel, about fifty yards away, but Derek had ducked behind the boulder and was out of sight. Where had he gone to?

Something above Nancy blocked out the watery Irish sunshine. There was a whistling sound in the air. She looked up.

A huge chunk of ancient stone was tumbling straight toward Nancy.

11

Over the Edge

Nancy twisted her body and sprang to the right to avoid the falling rock. It just missed grazing her left shoulder.

As her right foot landed, she came down at an angle on a broken bit of stone. Her ankle buckled, and she fell sideways. She tried to break her fall, but her shoe slid on a crumbling patch of dirt and shot out into open air, over the rim of the cliff.

Nancy clutched at the ground behind her. Her fingers closed on an upthrust rock and hung on tight.

The falling stone crashed on another rock, jolted and tumbled a few feet, then disappeared over the cliff. Holding on, Nancy cautiously peered over the edge.

Three hundred feet below, the ocean sparkled, cold and gray. There was a distant splash as the boulder plunged into the sea.

That could have been me, Nancy realized.

She twisted around to see where the stone had come from. The jagged fragment of wall sat there, impassive, grass sprouting from its cracks. A coating of mud showed where the fallen stone had been dislodged.

A stone cemented in place by soil doesn't just fall, Nancy thought. *Somebody pushed it.*

Nancy sprawled, shaking with relief, on the grass. Bob came rushing over. "Are you okay? Terry said he saw a falling rock nearly hit you."

"The rock missed me, thank goodness," Nancy said, rubbing her sore ankle. "But Bob, that stone has been there for centuries. Why would it fall today?" *And was it just coincidence that Terry was there to see it fall?* she added silently.

"Well, so long as you're all right," Bob said hurriedly. "Come over to the picnic and rest."

Nancy bit her lip. Why was Bob so blind to the fact that danger was dogging the tour?

George and Bess reached Nancy, with Rachel, Natalie, and Carl trotting up behind. Nancy looked around for Derek. He stood off to the side with Rhonda, muttering something in her ear.

Derek was near by just before that rock fell, too, Nancy reminded herself. She cast Derek a searching look. He simply turned away.

Fingers flying over the strings, a young fiddler sent a merry jig into the high-ceilinged community hall. Percussion was provided by the feet of a dozen dancers in black leather slippers and short black skirts, executing the skirling motions of a traditional Irish step dance.

"How young do you think that little girl is?" Bess wondered, pointing to the smallest dancer in the troupe. Barely four feet tall, she had the round face of a six- or seven-year-old. Her dark curls bobbed frantically as she hopped up and down to the music, eyes straight ahead. "She must have taken up stepping as soon as she could walk, to be this good already," Bess marveled.

Forehead furrowed, George studied the dancers' moves. "I can't believe how high they get their knees up. And see how they hold their upper bodies totally rigid, arms down at their sides? It must take perfect balance to move that way."

Rhonda, sitting on the wooden bench behind theirs, leaned forward. "It's even harder to do than it looks," she said. "With all the Irish folk in Australia, step dancing's popular, and I used to take lessons. I was a dismal failure, no joke."

Nancy answered with a thin smile. Rhonda had been clinging to her like a bur ever since they'd left the fort. With Rhonda around, Nancy could hardly investigate anyone's room at tonight's inn. Nancy recalled Derek confiding something to Rhonda that afternoon. Had he told her about finding Nancy in the hotel this morning? Was that why Rhonda suddenly wouldn't leave her alone?

The fiddler ended the song with a sharp downward stroke of his bow, and the dancers smartly stamped their feet together. The crowd burst into raucous clapping.

The leader of the troupe stepped forward, beaming. "Thank you very much," she called out as the clapping dwindled. "Now, it's not fair for us to have all the fun, is it? Who else would like to get their bones a-moving and their hearts a-pumping?" Hands flew up around the room. "Come on, gents as well as ladies," she coaxed the crowd.

Benches were pushed back to clear space on the linoleum floor, and the dancers fanned out to work with small groups of visitors. Nancy, George, Bess, and Rhonda, along with a couple of women from another tour group, teamed up with a raven-haired dancer named Moira. Lining up behind her, they copied her steps in slow motion. "Tap step, tap step, tap step, hop!" she called out. Pivoting around, she watched her pupils copy the steps. Nancy's mind was wiped clear of everything but the effort to dance. She found that as soon as she got her feet moving right, she forgot to keep her spine straight. When she got her back and feet together, she'd realize her arms were swinging outward for balance. She caught Bess's eye, and they both giggled.

George frowned at them and executed a tap-pivot-step move. "Arms straight down—but no fists," Moira advised George. She laid her hands flat against her thighs, fingers pointing down. "Like so. And don't hunch your shoulders."

Bess and Nancy traded glances and went into another giggle fit.

After an hour of tapping, stepping, and hopping, the visitors were glad to collapse back onto the benches and watch the trained dancers perform again. "Now I *really* appreciate how hard it is," George said to Nancy as the dance troupe launched into an intricate routine, pairing up, forming wheels, weaving lines together.

Nancy grinned and nodded, but as she turned her head she noticed Camilla leaving the hall by a side door. Nancy searched the crowd for Derek. She saw him leaning against a side wall, head close to Rachel's, murmuring in a low voice. Rachel smiled and blushed, and Derek bent closely toward her.

Nancy bit her lip. Which Selkirk was Derek interested in—Rhonda or Rachel? And how dare he hit on Rachel here, with Camilla looking on?

The night air felt cool against their flushed faces as they walked back through the village to their inn. George whistled a reel while Bess hopped and skipped along, but Nancy was quiet and distracted. She was keenly aware that Rhonda, Rachel, and Derek were walking arm-in-arm only a few steps behind them.

They soon reached the inn, a restored farmhouse overlooking one of Connemara's largest lakes, Lough Corrib. Nancy managed to smile as they said good night to the sisters and Derek, but she felt sour inside.

"So much for investigating," Nancy burst out, kicking off her shoes as they entered their bedroom. "And just when the case is heating up."

"My theory looks more likely all the time," George declared. "Someone's sabotaging the tour. One incident every day—and you're the latest victim, Nancy."

"Maybe so, George," Nancy said. "Rachel was nearby, but not that near. You know, both Derek and Terry know I was poking around the hotel this morning. What if one of them pushed that boulder at me as a warning not to snoop?"

Bess shivered. "I hate to think that."

"So do I," Nancy agreed. "But whoever the target

is, dangerous things are happening. And I don't think it'll stop unless we do something."

She picked up her daypack and took out the newspaper she'd found that morning in the Selkirks' room. She scanned the splashy front-page photo of a blond woman and an English football star, cringing from the prying cameras.

Bess peered over her shoulder. "Yuck, Nancy!" she exclaimed. "The *London Enquirer.* Did you really buy that sleazy paper? From what I see, those British rags are worse than supermarket scandal sheets in the States. Tacky celebrity gossip and hardly anything else."

Nancy shrugged. "I didn't buy it. I found it in Rhonda and Rachel's room this morning." She flipped the page. "Let's figure out why *they* were reading it. It may lead us to something."

She spread the paper on the bed, and the three girls lay side by side, poring over the columns of grubby print. Nancy's hopes faded as they turned one page after another.

Then George cried, "That's it!" She pointed to a small article at the bottom of a page.

Nancy frowned. "'Pop Star Breaks Down On Stage'? What's that got to do with the Selkirks?"

"It's not what it says, it's who it's by." George tapped her finger by the author's name.

Nancy and Bess gasped. "By Derek Thorogood,

London Enquirer Staff," the byline read.

"That sneak!" Nancy spluttered.

"So that's why he was snooping around Rhonda and Rachel's room," George said.

"If they've read this paper, they must know who he is now," Bess reasoned.

"Maybe not," Nancy said. "The article's buried so deep, they might not have seen it."

"It's true, they still seemed friendly with Derek tonight," George remarked.

Forehead creased in thought, Nancy considered this new twist. "But why? Why would a reporter be interested in the Selkirks? Who are they?"

"Spoiled rich girls from Australia," George suggested.

"That's not newsworthy enough," Nancy said. She drummed her fingers on the bed. "We need to do some research on them."

"But how?" Bess said. "We're in a tiny village in the middle of Connemara."

"Nothing's too far from anywhere else in Ireland," Nancy said. "We were in Galway City just this morning. It's got a university—there must be a library and cyber cafés there."

Bess looked doubtful. "We can't all three ditch the tour and go back to Galway City. Derek would notice, and so would Rhonda and Rachel."

"That's why we're not all going," Nancy said. "But

if one slips away . . ." She looked hopefully at Bess. "You're so good at research, Bess."

"Whoa, not me," Bess protested. "Go an extra day's ride out of the way?"

"It was a full day's ride along the coast," Nancy said, "but by the inland road it's not so far. Please, Bess?"

Rhonda and Rachel sat on one side of the breakfast room, dawdling over their streaky bacon and buttered toast the next morning. Rhonda kept glancing over at the table where Nancy and George sat. Bess had already slipped away to ride back to Galway City.

"I don't think they'll leave until we do," George murmured to Nancy. "They must know you're waiting to search their room."

Nancy grimaced and got to her feet. "Then we might as well go ride," she said. "But while they're so busy being suspicious of us, Derek could be upstairs pawing through their stuff."

"I can't believe they trust him more than they do you," George said as she and Nancy walked out into the front hall. "You're out to help them; he's out to dig up dirt on them."

Loud footsteps told them someone was coming down the stairs. They looked up to see Camilla, pouting, as she strapped on her helmet.

"Do you know where Derek is?" Nancy inquired in a casual voice.

"Derek? Ha!" Camilla replied. Her voice curled with scorn, and her eyes blazed. "Don't worry, Derek's gone—for good."

12

Vanished!

Nancy froze in surprise. "Derek's gone?"

With a huffy sigh, Camilla strode out into the paved courtyard. Nancy and George followed. "I found a note this morning," Camilla explained. "He checked out last night. By now he's at Shannon, waiting to fly to London to file his story."

"What story?" George asked.

Camilla checked over her shoulder whether anyone was listening. "I'll tell you as we ride."

The three girls quickly mounted their bikes and cruised away from the hotel. Once they were on the road, Camilla continued. "Derek came on this tour for one reason only: to do a smear job on the Selkirks."

"But why? Who are they?" George asked.

"Their father's Jacob Selkirk." George and Nancy looked blank. She added, "The media tycoon?"

"Never heard of him," Nancy admitted.

"Well, he started out in Australia," Camilla said, "but he's been buying newspapers in the U.K. over the past five years. He's as ruthless as they come. Last year he bought the *Clarion*—Derek's old paper, a top London daily. Right away Selkirk sacked a third of the staff, including Derek."

"So Derek hates him," Nancy guessed.

Camilla snorted. "I'll say. Derek was out of work for ages, till he finally got this post on that horrid rag the *London Enquirer*. Derek hates it. He'll never forgive Selkirk."

"So he decided to use the *London Enquirer* to get revenge?" George said.

"Spot on," Camilla said. "You see, Rhonda and Rachel were in London last winter. Every party they went to, every date they had, was covered in the tabloids. They certainly like to carry on—especially Rhonda. My friend's a McElheney agent in London and she tipped off Derek about the girls booking this tour. Derek decided to follow them and try to get an incriminating story. Or photo."

"So that's why he had that telephoto lens," Nancy murmured. "The ultimate snoop equipment."

"Too bad he's such an amateur photographer." Camilla sneered. "Not a single picture came out."

"But the Selkirks didn't carry on," George said. "Except to let Derek flirt with them."

Camilla rolled her eyes. "You noticed, eh? Derek said he was flirting to lead them into misbehaving. I played along. But then he started to enjoy it; he liked seeing the sisters compete for him. We had an awful row about it last night."

"And that's why he left?" George asked.

"Sort of. But really," Camilla admitted, "I just think he was tired of cycling, and tired of waiting for a story to materialize."

"So what will he write?" Nancy wondered.

Camilla sighed. "I suspect he'll just make something up, which could be even worse."

Nancy considered this new twist. Had Derek really left—or had he just told Camilla so? And if he was gone, would the danger stop?

Today's route lay along the wide lake called Lough Corrib. Terry had dropped off box lunches at a grassy picnic area on the lakeshore. Carl, Jim, Natalie, and Bob were already there eating when the girls rode up.

"I don't get the point of fly-fishing," Natalie was saying, motioning upshore toward the tiny figures of anglers standing thigh-deep in the lake. "They never move. How is that a sport?"

"It's a great way to get in touch with nature," Carl remarked.

"Plus, you end up with fresh grilled trout for lunch," Jim said, with a discouraged look at his thin ham sandwich. "Sounds good to me."

Nancy opened her box lunch, but she glanced back up the road, unspooling far across the level, brown-green moors. Rhonda and Rachel should have caught up with them by now. But she didn't want to say anything that would prod Bob into taking a head count. No point in making it obvious that Bess wasn't with the group today.

When Natalie announced that she and Jim were opting for the shorter route that afternoon, Camilla and Carl decided to join them. As the four cyclists were leaving, Bob got a call on his cell phone. "Right, run back and get her, then go up to Cashkellmara," Nancy heard him say. "Call back and let me know how it goes."

Bob flipped his phone shut. "That was Terry," he informed Nancy and George. "Rachel called for a pickup. I guess that means Rhonda's with them. We'll leave their lunches here in case they stop by later. So, shall we ride on together?"

"Fine," said Nancy, moving toward their bikes. "Hey, we heard that Derek went home."

Bob sighed. "I know. It's just as well. Now maybe the tour will be peaceful again."

Nancy responded quickly. "Why? Do you think he's behind all these accidents?"

Bob paused, perplexed. "Why, no. What makes you think that? I just meant he's such a ladies' man, I was afraid a fight would break out. What do you mean, all these 'accidents'?"

"Well, Rhonda passing out, Rachel getting hit by a sign, a car running them off the road," Nancy said. "The van hitting George . . ."

"Not to mention the rock falling at Nancy yesterday," George added.

Bob grimaced as he straddled his bike. "No one's been hurt."

"Luckily," Nancy replied, shivering at the memory of her close shave. As they pushed off, she added, "Frankly, Bob, I'm worried. We know who Rhonda and Rachel's dad is. What if somebody's out to hurt them? Shouldn't you bring in the police?"

Bob fell silent, gazing steadily between his handlebars. "Rhonda and Rachel insisted," he finally said. "That was their main condition when they signed up. No bodyguards, no publicity."

"It may be too late for that," George said. "Did you know Derek's from the *London Enquirer*?"

"A tabloid reporter?" Bob gaped. "Oh, this tour is a nightmare. I'll be lucky to keep my job." He looked at the darkening sky. "Here comes one of those famous Irish rain showers. Hurry up—let's get to the village over the hill."

Nancy, George, and Bob soon whizzed into a quiet

cluster of whitewashed buildings. They stashed their bikes and ran inside the nearest shop, just as the clouds broke open.

Rain drummed on the roof as Nancy and George admired piles of thick cable-knit sweaters in a soft off-white yarn. "Those are handmade by Aran Islanders," Bob said. "They're incredibly warm."

"And beautiful," George said, holding one up. "I'm definitely buying one."

"You'll need it tonight," Bob said. "We're staying on an island, in an old monastery. It's been restored, but it's still drafty."

"How do we get to the island?" Nancy asked.

"There's a road built out to it, on an old stone jetty," Bob said. "But when the tide comes in, the sea covers the road and you're cut off."

"How romantic!" George exclaimed. But Nancy, picking out a sweater for her dad, thought that romantic isolation might not be so good right now.

The old monastery's crumbling stone walls and tall, arched windows did look poetic, Nancy thought as she wheeled over the causeway to the tiny island. Inside, however, the place had been fitted up in complete modern style. Nancy and George were happy to find Bess snuggled by a fireplace in the lounge. "I'm glad you're back," she said, popping up. "I caught a bus from Galway City; they took my bike on the roof."

Nancy unzipped her windbreaker. "Any luck?"

Bess nodded excitedly and sat forward on the couch. "You'll never guess who Rhonda and Rachel's father is," she confided.

"Jacob Selkirk, Australian media magnate," George replied, plopping down beside her.

Bess looked hurt. "How did you know?"

"Camilla," Nancy said, perching on the arm of the sofa. "Derek was fired from a Selkirk paper, and he came on the tour to get a dirty scoop on the girls. But he gave up and left last night."

Bess shook her head. "Still, he wouldn't want to hurt them. But someone else does. Listen to this: Jacob Selkirk's newspaper, the *Sydney Examiner*, cracked a big Australian crime ring last fall. Ever since, the family's been receiving death threats."

George whistled. "So that's why Rhonda and Rachel lived in London last winter—for safety."

Just then, they heard Rhonda in the entry hall. "What do you mean, you don't know where she is?" she demanded. "What sort of security do you call that?"

"Look, Rhonda," they heard Bob's sharp reply, "you want total security? Hire a bodyguard."

"Have you ever *had* a bodyguard?" Rhonda shot back. "It's such a downer. No thanks!"

Nancy saw Bob in the doorway, wearily rubbing his temples. "Terry said Rachel called for a repair.

He was going to pick her up. He's not answering his cell phone, though. I called the bike shop in Cashkellmara to see if Terry and Rachel had arrived, but there's no answer there. I'll try Rachel's cell again." He unclipped his phone from his belt and dialed. The girls heard an answering ring outside. Bob perked up. "I hear her!"

Rhonda flushed. "Uh, no—that's on my bike. I kept the cell phone when I went on my own."

Bob's eyes began to bug out. "You rode away and left her without communication? Stranded with a broken bike at the side of the road?"

Nancy saw Rhonda's eyes fill with tears. "It wasn't broken then! Look, we had an argument. She got mad and rode away, and I happened to have the phone. Oh, where is she now?"

Nancy rose from the couch. After hearing Bess's news, she understood Rhonda's panic. Were Australian criminals stalking the Selkirks?

She broke into their conversation. "I remember seeing the bike shop when we rode through Cashkellmara. I'd be happy to ride back and check it out."

For once, Rhonda looked glad about Nancy's interference. "Thanks, Nancy, that'd be great."

"Better hurry, though," Bob told Nancy. "It's already three-thirty. The tide comes in soon. By five-ten, the causeway will be impassable. While you're gone, I'll call the local Garda and ask if any road accidents have been reported."

Nancy cycled back across the causeway, gazing uneasily at the encroaching waters on either side. She was well down the road on the mainland before she realized she hadn't taken a cell phone. In order to make it back across the causeway safely, though, she couldn't turn back.

Studying the map, Nancy spotted a small inland road that seemed the most direct route to Cashkell-mara. She swung onto it and cycled steadily.

Then she saw a spot of red beside the road up ahead.

Nancy pedaled hard, feeling a lump in her throat. The closer she got, the more sure she was of what it could be.

It was the McElheney van, half overturned in a muddy ditch.

As Nancy approached, she spotted tire tracks on the banks of the ditch, half washed out by the recent rainfall. Terry must have crashed shortly after he had called Bob, Nancy realized; the rain had started soon after the call. But the tracks headed north. Rachel's breakdown had been south of here. Where had Terry been going?

Parking her bike, Nancy went to inspect the van. The passenger side door was jammed against a mound of dirt, but the driver's side door had been forced open a couple feet. She looked inside gingerly. No bodies—that was good—but there was a splatter of blood on the dashboard. She touched it. It was still sticky and fresh.

Beside the gearshift the mobile phone sat in its bracket. Nancy took it out and tried to turn it on, but the battery had gone dead.

She went around to the dented back door and opened it. The back of the van was empty; no magenta bike waiting for a repair.

Nancy began to search the immediate area. A set of large footprints led away from the van, clear in the mud. Only one pair, weaving from side to side. One person had walked this way, unsteadily . . . maybe dazed from the crash. *If these are Terry's footprints, he didn't have Rachel with him,* Nancy thought. As the prints reached the surrounding bracken they disappeared, leaving no impression on the tough sod.

Nancy frowned. If she had a cell phone, she could call Bob, or the police. Now she'd have to ride for help. She hadn't passed any houses along this road. That meant the monastery on the island was the nearest help. She jumped on her bike again and rode north a quarter mile or so.

Then she screeched to a halt. There was a second pair of tire tracks in the mud. But if a passerby had stopped to help Terry, why were these tracks so far from the wrecked van?

Nancy straddled her bike. These were smaller tires, probably a car's. Several muddy footsteps, all jumbled together, covered the pavement near the tracks, as if there had been a scuffle. Then the car tracks made a U-turn, heading south. These last tracks were sharply pressed in the mud, as if they'd been made later, after the rain.

There was no time to lose. Nancy sped back to the island, anxiously checking her watch. It was five minutes past five when she reached the causeway. The road looked like a paved strip of ocean, water rising to the top of its stone banks.

Nancy licked her lips. The causeway was only half a mile long—surely she could cover that distance in five minutes. But the seawater was considerably rougher than it had been earlier. Already the highest waves splashed onto the road.

And what if the rainstorm today made the water higher than usual? Nancy wondered tensely. Would the road stay clear long enough for her to reach the island?

13

Too Late?

Cursing herself for forgetting the cell phone, Nancy knew she had no choice but to ride on across the causeway to the island. She pushed off, hearing an ominous splatter beneath her wheels.

She swerved sideways to avoid a wave. Her wheels slid in a patch of brackish mud at the road's edge. Nancy's heart lurched as the bike tipped sideways toward the cold, roiling sea.

Nancy threw her body to the side and pulled hard on the handlebars. Somehow she managed to wrench her wheels back onto the slick pavement.

A few yards farther on, Nancy began to lose heart. She threw a glance over her shoulder to check out an escape route. But the road behind her was already submerged under a thin sheet of lapping tidewater.

Nancy stood up on the pedals, hearing a slushy whirr as her wheels spun. She was almost halfway across now. She plunged on, feeling her wheels grow increasingly unstable.

The water began to splash under her pedals, and she had to fight to make the wheels turn. Desperate, she jumped off the bike, sloshing through water up to her mid-calves. She covered the last several yards dragging her bike behind her in the water.

Stumbling up the final slope, Nancy turned to look behind her. The causeway was now completely underwater. She had made it, but just barely.

Wet and exhausted, Nancy staggered across the green lawn and into the monastery. She followed the cheery sound of familiar voices echoing off stone. Pushing open a stout oak door, she walked into the monks' ancient dining hall.

The rest of the tour group, gathered around a long plank table, stared at her as if she were a ghost. "Nancy, you got across!" Bess exclaimed.

"I thought you'd missed it for sure," Bob said. "We were waiting for you to call. I was afraid you'd have to find a place to stay on the mainland."

Nancy nodded and croaked, "I couldn't call. I forgot to take a phone. But I found the van—crashed by the side of the road."

Rhonda leaped up, her hand anxiously at her throat. "Rachel?"

Nancy shook her head. "No sign of her, or of Terry."

"A crash?" Bob spluttered angrily. "That Terry! He's had a couple of accidents before—little stuff, like that brush with George the other morning. But he was on a warning. Good thing he'd already delivered the luggage before he went to collect Rachel."

Rhonda wheeled to face Bob. "That's all you care about—the luggage? What about my sister?"

Bob cringed.

Nancy quickly interjected, "It looked like Terry might have been hurt. There was some blood on the dashboard, and one set of footprints leading away. Another car had stopped nearby, where there were more footprints. Someone else may have driven Rachel away."

Rhonda turned deadly pale.

Nancy crossed her arms. "Rhonda, is there something you're not telling us?"

Rhonda drew a deep breath. "Well, to start with . . . Rachel's bike didn't break down."

"But I saw her—" Jim began.

"That was me," Rhonda said. "I jammed my own bike's gears to make Rachel ride on without me. My plan was to wait for Derek Thorogood so I could ride with him."

Camilla narrowed her eyes. "Derek left this morning."

121

"Well, I didn't know that then, did I?" Rhonda declared. "Anyway, Rachel rode off, calling me a drongo and a boofhead and all sorts of names." She swallowed hard. "And that—that was the last I saw of her."

Nancy faced Rhonda. "Do you have any idea what may have happened to her?"

Rhonda nodded slowly. "When I was sitting there—waiting for Derek—I saw that blue car drive past."

"The same one that tried to run you off the road?" George asked.

Rhonda hesitated. "It went so fast, I couldn't be sure. But"—she dropped her eyes—"if it was who I think it was . . ."

"Rhonda, you've got to come clean with us now," Nancy said. "You know who was driving that car, don't you?"

"Yes," Rhonda said in a choked voice. "It was Stewart Smithson."

"Who's that?"

"He works for our father—at least, he used to, back in Sydney," Rhonda said. "He was our driver for a few months. When he showed up here in Ireland, he contacted me and told me Daddy had sent him to watch us."

"But I thought you didn't want a bodyguard," Bob said.

"That was mostly Rachel," Rhonda said. "She had

122

a huge argument with Daddy about it. She wants to live a normal life without guards. I can see her point, but I could see Dad's, too. Rachel whinged and grizzled about the bodyguards all last winter in London, until Dad got bloody tired of it. It made sense to me that he'd send Smithson on the sly."

She hung her head. "I guess I should have phoned Dad to check on Smithson's story. But we did know the man. And Smithson said he'd be discreet about it so Rache wouldn't know."

Nancy arched an eyebrow. "So that was who I saw you talking to in the alley that morning—the same man I saw at Shannon, and again in Galway? The one with the missing finger?"

Rhonda winced. "Yes. The one you asked me about, who I said I didn't know. I didn't want you to tell Rachel he was about!"

"But he clearly wasn't guarding you very well," Nancy argued. "That very first night here, you drank that bad soda—"

"That was a fake," Rhonda admitted, lifting her chin almost defiantly. "Smithson suggested we should frighten Rachel so she'd agree to have a bodyguard. So I pretended to pass out after sipping Rachel's soda."

"There was nothing in the soda?" Carl asked.

"Nothing at all," Rhonda said.

So it didn't matter that Terry had spilled the soda,

Nancy reflected. That was an innocent accident after all.

"What about the falling sign the next night?" Jim wondered.

Rhonda gritted her teeth. "That was a setup, too. I slipped Rachel a note to lure her outside the pub so Smithson could rig up an accident." She grimaced. "I didn't expect her to get hurt. When I talked to Smithson in the alley the next morning, he said the sign fell wrong. It was supposed to go in the other direction and miss her . . . or so he said."

"So later that day, when Smithson ran you off the road . . . ?" Nancy asked.

Rhonda nodded. "I knew he was going to do that, too. But he drove at us so hard, it finally scared me. That's why I switched bikes with Rachel, so I could go on to Galway City. I paged Smithson and arranged to meet him. That's when I told him to clear off for good."

"And did he?" Nancy asked.

"I thought he did," Rhonda replied. "He seemed to be gone. But I felt embarrassed that I'd helped him. That's why I kept close watch on you, Nancy, so you wouldn't learn about it. I knew you were suspicious. But I figured it was over."

Rhonda swallowed hard, and her eyes filled with tears. "Now Rachel's disappeared. What if Smithson caught up with her?"

Bob cleared his throat. "Rhonda, I think you'd better go call your father."

"Yes, you've got to find out if Smithson was really working for him," Nancy pointed out.

Rhonda nodded and walked out, footsteps dragging. Nancy sank into the nearest chair. The members of the group traded shocked glances in silence.

George broke the silence. "So it was Smithson who pushed that rock at you yesterday, Nancy."

Nancy saw a panicked look cross Camilla's face. "Uh . . . no, that was Derek," Camilla said.

Everyone swiveled to look at Camilla in surprise. "I saw him do it from a distance," she admitted. "I confronted him about it last night—that was what started our row. He told me he thought you were on to him, Nancy, and he wanted to stop you. But the rock came so close, it frightened him. It really did— you've got to believe that. He's not a bad bloke; he didn't mean to hurt anybody. That's a big part of why he left."

Just then they heard a stricken cry from the hallway outside. Nancy jumped up and ran out.

She saw Rhonda standing by the front desk, cradling the telephone receiver against her chest.

"What is it?" Nancy asked.

Rhonda turned numbly to face her. "Daddy says . . . he says he's received a ransom note from Smithson."

Nancy gasped.

Rhonda's face crumpled as she clattered the phone back on the hook. "He says he's got Rachel hidden somewhere in the Irish countryside," she forced out through her sobs. "And he wants three million dollars for her!"

14

Whereabouts Unknown

Nancy felt herself trembling at the awful news. So Rachel had been kidnapped!

She threw her arms around Rhonda and helped her walk back to the dining hall. One look at everyone's face told her that they had all heard Rhonda's announcement.

"Oh, Nancy!" Rhonda burst out. "You're a detective—you've got to help!"

Nancy sensed another wave of surprise run through Bob, Carl, Jim, Natalie, and Camilla. "A detective?" Camilla gasped.

Nancy lowered Rhonda into her chair. "Yes, a detective," she admitted. She traded glances with Bess and George, signaling to them that it was okay to reveal her secret. "I'm here on vacation, not on a case.

But yes, that's what I do. I'm strictly an amateur, of course."

"So that's why you were asking me so many questions," Bob said.

Nancy nodded. "Trouble kept breaking out, and I wanted to get to the bottom of it," she said, "to ensure our safety. And I wanted to protect Rachel and Rhonda—only they wouldn't let me."

Rhonda laid her head on her arms. "I thought things were under control. I thought Smithson was helping us!"

Nancy drew a breath. "I don't hold grudges, Rhonda," she said. "I want to do whatever I can to help. There's only one problem: I can't get off the island to begin investigating."

"I suppose we could call to the mainland for someone to pick you up in a boat," Bob suggested. "But it'll be dark soon. Maybe you should wait until tomorrow morning."

Nancy bit her lip. "Smithson's trail will be cold by then," she said. "He's a clever man—he's gotten away from me before. Bob, at least we should call the Garda."

"I already did, to ask if there were any roadside crashes," Bob reminded her. "But I'll call again."

"Listen!" Nancy hushed him, holding up one finger. "What's that?"

From outside came the grinding sound of a boat

cutting through the water. Nancy jumped to her feet and headed for the hotel's front door. The rest of the group followed close behind.

In the gathering dusk they could see a speedboat churning through the water between the island and the mainland. On its steel sides were painted the symbol of the Irish Garda.

A plainclothes officer standing in the stern of the boat was the first to hop off as it reached shore. "I'm looking for Bob Prendergast," he said.

Bob stepped forward. "That's me."

"Keith Mulryan," the officer introduced himself. "Special investigations." He flipped open a wallet to show his Garda identification.

"Boy, are we glad to see you," Bob said. "One of the members of our tour group is missing."

"Yes, Miss Rachel Selkirk," Mulryan said.

Bob gaped. "How did you know?"

Mulryan allowed himself a tiny smile. "We already knew you were missing your van and driver—Terry O'Leary, was it? Then Jacob Selkirk called to report he'd received a ransom note for Rachel."

Rhonda blew out a sigh of relief. "When Daddy makes a call, the law springs into action fast."

Mulryan looked over at her. "Are you the other Miss Selkirk?" Rhonda nodded. "I'd like a word with you and Mr. Prendergast."

Rhonda grabbed Nancy by the shoulders and

pushed her forward. "You should talk to Nancy first. She's a detective from the States, and she's been watching Rachel all along. She knew something was up."

Mulryan raised his eyebrows. "A detective? Well, that's a bit of luck for us."

"I hope I can help," Nancy said modestly.

"Your man O'Leary," Mulryan said, turning to Bob, "we think we're closing in on him. The van was found abandoned in the vicinity of—"

"Cashkellmara," Nancy finished his sentence. "I saw the site of the accident. His footprints went off into the bracken—he must be wandering about in a daze. He'll need medical attention, but don't arrest him."

Mulryan looked surprised. "But I thought he was our suspected kidnapper."

"Footprints show he was in the van alone when it crashed," Nancy explained. "Besides, we have a stronger suspect: a man named Stewart Smithson. He knew Rachel Selkirk and had already made a couple of attempts to hurt her."

Mulryan gave a low whistle and pulled out a notebook. "Can you give me a description of him?"

"About six feet tall, weight around two hundred pounds," Nancy estimated. "I'd say he's around thirty-five or forty years old. Short brown hair, dark eyes, ruddy complexion, Australian accent. He wears a black wool overcoat. Oh, and here's your identifying clincher: He's missing the little finger on his left hand."

"I'll radio out the description immediately," said Mulryan eagerly. "This is great."

"He may be driving a late-model blue sedan," Nancy said. "And—wait a minute." She ran over to her bike and dug out of her daypack pocket the paper on which George had written Smithson's license number. She ran back to the officer and handed it to him. "That'll help," she said.

Mulryan broke out into a grin. "It certainly will. This is the break we've been waiting for!"

"Officer, Nancy knows a lot about the case," Rhonda said. "I think you should take her with you to the mainland. She could identify Smithson if he's found."

"His car, too," Nancy added.

"And she'd be a friendly face for Rachel to see if she's found," Bob said.

"*When* she's found," Mulryan said with a confident smile. "I'd be happy to let you join us, Nancy. You've got a trained eye; that's always a help in any investigation."

Mulryan introduced a junior officer, Liam Murphy, who would stay on the island and conduct interviews while Mulryan rejoined the manhunt. Meanwhile, the speedboat driver radioed to the mainland the information Nancy had given them.

George disappeared for a moment and came back with the Aran Isle sweater Nancy had bought earlier that day. "You'll need this; it'll be cold out on the water, now that night is falling," George reminded Nancy. "I'm sure your dad won't mind if you wear it before he does."

Nancy grinned. "Thanks, George."

Soon the speedboat was cutting back across the channel, heading for Cashkellmara. A fine, cold sea spray spritzed Nancy as they flew along. She shivered, grateful for the warm sweater.

Even before they landed, Nancy could see a squad car waiting, its lights flashing. "We've got O'Leary," called out another plainclothes officer, standing by the car's open door. "You want to go talk to him?"

Mulryan nodded and ushered Nancy into the car. With a warning burp of their siren, they tore up the road. "He wandered into a café up in Cashkellmara," the second officer, Danny McGrath, reported. "Five or six miles from the crash site. He's not making a whole lot of sense, but maybe he can tell us something."

The front window of the simple roadside café was brightly lit as they drove up. Nancy followed the officers inside.

Terry O'Leary sat at a Formica-topped table, hands

cupped around a steaming mug of milky tea. His shaggy hair was damp, the curls plastered against his neck. Mud and grime streaked his face and hands. His gray pullover sweater was ripped and spattered with mud; small burs and brambles clung to the legs of his corduroy trousers.

A police officer was putting salve on the wound on Terry's forehead. "Augh, man, you're killing me!" Terry cried out, flinching in pain.

The officer clucked. "That's a nasty gash you've got, and no mistake," he warned Terry. "Be sure to keep a clean dressing on it, d'ya hear?"

Terry moaned softly in reply. He opened his eyes again. Seeing Nancy, he stiffened. "No, don't tell me . . . is Bob here?"

Nancy shook her head, sitting down across the table from Terry. "He's with the group at the hotel. Are you okay?"

"Don't tell him I wrecked the van," Terry said, clearly agitated. "He said he'd sack me if I crashed another one."

Nancy laid a gentle hand on his wrist. "Bob already knows about the accident," she told him. "But he'll be glad to hear you're not badly hurt. The important thing right now is to find Rachel."

Terry gave a groggy blink. "Rachel?"

"Yes. Didn't she call you to come get her for a repair?"

Terry stared vaguely at Nancy, as if trying to focus his mind. "Rachel . . . Rachel. No, she never called me. Somebody else did . . . a man."

"Jim de Fusco?" Nancy suggested. "He told me he'd called you about Rhonda. But she didn't need any help; she, er, fixed her gears herself. I thought you also told Bob that Rachel had called. I was there when he took the call."

Terry hung his head. "That's what I told Bob. But that was a bit of a cover story. You see, I . . . I stopped in a pub for a wee bit. Not for a drink, mind you, just to watch the football on television. Soccer, you call it." He looked away from Nancy to the surrounding officers, as if asking for support. "It's a very important match."

"Aye," one of the officers verified.

"I didn't take my mobile inside," Terry admitted. "The battery was dead—it only worked when it was powered by the car's engine. So when Jim called, I thought maybe Rachel had tried to phone while I was in the pub."

"You mean Rhonda," Nancy corrected him.

Terry blinked, "Rhonda, Rachel—I always get them mixed up. It must have been Rhonda I was after. But I didn't want Bob to know I'd stopped at the pub," he said sheepishly, "so I told him Rachel had called me herself."

Nancy squeezed her eyes shut in frustration. So

Terry's whereabouts had been a red herring; a clue that went nowhere. All along it had been Rhonda he'd gone to pick up, not Rachel. And meanwhile, what had Stewart Smithson been up to?

Terry was still rambling on. "I drove to where Jim told me she was, but she was gone. I turned around and drove back north—a long ways, it seemed like. It had just started to rain when I spotted her riding way ahead. I reckoned she'd fixed the bike herself."

"Think carefully. Was it Rhonda or Rachel?" Nancy asked.

Terry tried to concentrate for a moment, then winced with pain. "Don't know for sure. All I know is, a car came up behind me, real fast. With the rain and all, I didn't hear it at first. The next thing I knew, he was running me off the road."

Nancy sat up straight. "A blue sedan?"

Terry struggled to remember. "I think so. Like I said, it was raining, and I couldn't see so well. I looked in my mirrors . . ." His body sagged. "From then on, everything's a blank."

Nancy leaned back in her chair, frustrated. Was it Rhonda or Rachel that Terry had seen on the road? And if the driver of the blue car was Smithson . . .

Just then, a squawk rose from the radio clipped to Officer Mulryan's belt. He whipped it to his ear. "Mulryan," he said.

The dispatcher's voice came through, crackly with

static. "Keith, we've found the blue car. The license number matches and all. It's parked at the edge of the peat bog."

"Is Smithson in it?" Mulryan radioed back, throwing an excited look at Nancy.

"Negative, Keith," the radio voice replied. "But there *is* a magenta bicycle in the trunk."

15

The Bog Demon Awaits

"You're sure it's Smithson's car?" Mulryan asked.

The staticky voice answered, "Yeah. Same license and all."

"We'll be right there. Over." He clipped the radio back to his belt and gestured to Nancy and Danny. "Let's go to the bog and check it out."

As the Garda car hurtled through the velvety night, Mulryan thought aloud. "They must have left the car and gone on by foot."

Nancy considered this. "Maybe not. What if he got a second car? He must have known we'd be able to identify the blue one."

"In that case, he'd need an accomplice," Mulryan said, "to drive the other car here to pick him up. Well, I'll radio headquarters and have them phone round to nearby car hire agencies. We'll see if Smithson hired another car today."

"I doubt he'd use his real name to rent the car," Nancy reminded him. "Make sure they give the agencies his full description."

Mulryan nodded and radioed the message. After he was finished, he stared out through the window at the flat, featureless landscape approaching the bogland. "If they did go by foot, we'd have our work cut out. Tracing them through that bog would be a nightmare."

"What is a bog? Is it like a swamp?" Nancy asked, leaning forward from the rear seat.

Mulryan considered the question. "A bog is—well, it's a bog. The ground is soft and mucky for miles. The surface is what we call peat: a sort of gluey, dense soil. People cut it into chunks, cart it away, and let it dry into hard bricks to use for fuel. Most folk hereabouts heat their homes with peat fire."

"Of course, when people take away the peat, the bog just gets boggier," Danny McGrath added. "It's a fearsome place, all right. Some folks around here won't even drive on this bog road at night. They think evil spirits would jump out and attack their car." He grinned.

"But people can walk in it?" Nancy asked.

Mulryan shrugged. "There's no path, really—just a hundred little lanes, the boreens. They're like ridges of solid ground weaving around between the swampy bits. Even a local lad would have a devil of a time navigating it in the dark."

Swinging around the narrow roads, Nancy peered at road signs. It was hard in the dark to decipher the English names at the top, let alone the Gaelic ones below. But she could tell this wasn't the road she'd cycled over earlier.

As the next sign flashed past, Nancy called out, "What was that name?"

Danny McGrath said, "Clostermeade?"

Nancy straightened up. "I've heard that name before. . . ."

Danny shrugged. "It's nothing famous—just a wee village and a manor house."

"And the manor house is deserted," Keith Mulryan added. "The bog kept expanding and overtook the grounds. The house is practically cut off by now—no one goes near it."

Nancy snapped her fingers. "I remember! I heard Smithson talking about Clostermeade Manor. We were in a pottery shop in Galway City. He asked the sales clerk about the residence; he said his aunt used to work there as a maid."

McGrath looked over his shoulder. "Funny coincidence."

"My guess is he was lying," Nancy said. "He probably just said that to get more information from the woman. I suppose he'd cased out the area already and spotted this empty manor house. He'd want to learn more about it."

Keith Mulryan smacked a fist into the other palm. "That's it! It'd be a perfect place to hide out. Let's go."

They sped through the tiny village of Clostermeade. Mulryan pointed through to a hulking shadow on a low rise beyond the village. "That's the manor house. Pull over by the gates, Danny—just ahead, there."

Danny swung the car into a weed-choked paved area that looked like it had once been the foot of a driveway. A pair of rusted iron gates barred the old drive. Getting out of the car, Nancy examined the dilapidated wrought iron, its dented curlicues the evidence of a long-vanished grandeur.

"The blue car is about half a mile down this road," Danny said. "Should we go there first?"

Keith shook his head. "Smithson wasn't asking about Clostermeade Manor for nothing. I bet Nancy's right; Smithson's using this place as a hideout. Why don't you drive on and check out the car, Danny? Then run back here and meet us."

"Okay. But you'd better take the torch," Danny said, handing over a monster-sized flashlight. "It's not safe for us to go splitting up. This man may be armed and dangerous."

Keith gave a lopsided grin. "Then radio for some backup. We might as well make use of all the chaps from Dublin they're flying in for this." He snickered. "I guess they don't think we westerners can handle a high-stakes operation."

Danny snorted. "Well, we'll show them."

Nancy and Keith Mulryan got out of the car, and Danny drove away. Keith switched on his huge flashlight and played its beam over the old gates. "Shouldn't take much to get through here," he said. He reached out and touched the rusty lock on the gates. The lock plate fell to the side, and one gate tipped open, shifting on its hinges with a loud creak.

"Better turn off your flashlight," Nancy warned him. Privately, she wondered how many stakeouts Keith had been on in this rural area. Not many, she guessed. "If Smithson is up at the house, we don't want him to know we're coming."

"Aye," said Keith, "but we'll need light to get through the bog. The drive ends up ahead; the bog devoured it." He aimed the flashlight at the broken pavement ahead.

Keith strode forward, sweeping the beam from side to side but keeping it low. He halted at the end of the pavement. "There're ridges of packed soil. You've just got to find them," he whispered. He began to feel his way forward.

The darkness soon closed in around them, despite

Keith's flashlight. Nancy kept her eyes trained on the ground before her, setting one foot directly in front of the other. A quick glance to either side showed gleaming dark muck, with very little grass and absolutely no trees.

The deeper in they went, the bleaker it seemed. No sounds of birds or small animals, the usual signs of life in a normal landscape. Her senses keenly attuned, Nancy imagined she could almost hear the bog breathe.

Then Keith Mulryan disappeared from in front of her.

Nancy gasped and halted her steps. Her hands flew out, searching for Keith.

She heard a squelching, sucking sound a few feet to her left. "Keith?" She crouched, groping in that direction.

A sudden sharp breath broke out by her ankles. "I've gone down!" Mulryan panted.

Nancy reached out and felt mucky hands grasp her forearm. She braced her bent legs and started to pull backward. Mulryan was clawing desperately for a solid ridge.

Nancy's muscles ached with the tension of pulling the man upward. But she dared not step in the other direction for more leverage. The open bog gaped there, too, like quicksand.

With one final great heave, Mulryan hauled himself

onto the footpath. He sprawled gratefully on the packed dirt. "Just an encounter with the bog demon," he joked weakly.

Nancy helped him to his feet. "I'll go first for a while," she offered. "Until you've recovered." Mulryan nodded.

They moved more slowly now, Mulryan staying only a few inches behind Nancy. She felt her shoulders hunch with anxiety. If she made a false step, she might sink like Keith had.

"Well, if we're having trouble, that means Smithson and Rachel are, too," she said to herself grimly. Then, with a sinking heart, she reflected that they must have come through here in daylight. That would have been nothing compared to this.

At last, Nancy sensed a line of shrubbery a few yards ahead, breaking up the bleak flatness of the bog. She pushed toward it, still setting one foot carefully in front of the other.

As she got closer, she could see a light faintly wink between the tangled strands of foliage. Her pulse quickened. Surely that was the manor house getting near. Was someone in there? Was it—Smithson?

Behind her, Nancy heard Keith stumble to the side of the path. His boots squelched, and he swore under his breath. Nancy halted, but she heard him haul himself back onto the path. She pressed on.

Reaching the bushes, Nancy discovered that it was

a ragged, overgrown boxwood hedge. She fought to pry open a gap in it. Sharp twigs whipped her face and hands. Keith joined her and threw his body weight beside hers. They finally flattened a section enough to struggle over it.

Ahead of them stretched an expanse of grass. Nancy stepped slowly forward, testing the uneven ground of the old garden for soft patches.

In the darkness, Nancy resorted to an old trick she'd learned from wilderness survival training. Shutting her eyes, she cut off her dependence on the sense of sight. Her other senses now came more sharply into play. Every sound around her, every variation in the terrain, even the airflow created by neighboring objects, all were magnified as she moved silently forward.

Several yards behind her she could hear Keith's footsteps pause. There was a soft creak of leather as he fumbled for something on his belt. What was he doing? Now was not the time to—

Keith's muffled voice said, "Mulryan here. Any word on that backup?"

Then a loud hiss of static escaped from his radio. The dispatcher's voice squawked forth, "About six miles off yet, Keith."

Nancy whirled around, her heart in her mouth. This close to the house, silence was absolutely necessary. What was Keith thinking?

144

The low beam of the flashlight revealed the officer's startled face. Even he hadn't expected the volume on his radio to be set so high.

Behind her, Nancy heard a wooden shutter clatter open. A harsh square of light broke into the darkness for a moment, then was switched off.

Nancy dropped to her knees behind a broken stone bench. Keith crouched behind a weathered wooden arbor nearby. Nancy heard him draw his gun from its holster and click off the safety latch.

And at almost the same time, Nancy heard from the house the answering click of a gun.

A harsh Australian bray rose from the house. "Whoever it is, I know you're out there. I've got the girl here. Come any closer, and I'll shoot her."

16

The Luck of the Irish

Crouching behind the bench, Nancy raised her head just enough to see Smithson's face framed in a broken-out window of the manor house. He held Rachel in front of him, in a headlock. Her pale face looked twisted in sheer panic. Nancy's heart ached for her.

Smithson shifted his position, and a slash of moonlight fell across his face. Beads of sweat glittered on his forehead, but the hand that held the gun was steady.

Over in the arbor, Keith Mulryan leveled his gun at the kidnapper. "You might as well come out, Smithson," he called out. "We've got you covered. Don't hurt the girl and everything will be all right."

Smithson swiveled to face the arbor. Nancy spied her chance. In the darkness, she might be able to slip across the shadowy garden and get into the house. She stretched out one leg to the right and shifted her weight, making as little noise as possible.

"And who would you be, then?" Smithson fired a sarcastic question at Mulryan.

"Keith Mulryan, Galway Garda," the officer replied in a confident voice. "I've got men stationed all around the property. You'll never escape. You might as well surrender."

Bending low, Nancy took a few lunges and found cover behind a knee-high terrace wall. From there she crept on all fours toward the house. There was a door in the side wall. Not too far . . .

"Oh, yeah?" Smithson countered. "Don't play me for a mug. Where are these men of yours? Stuck in that blasted bog? I could barely get through in daylight, and it's pitch-black now. Sorry, but I'm not scared of you and your gutless bog-slogging colleagues." He snickered cruelly. "I've come a long way to get my hands on one of the Selkirks, and I'm not giving her up. Do you know how much money she's worth to me?"

Nancy stepped carefully onto the slate step and laid her hand on the doorknob.

"Do you know how many years in prison she's worth to you?" Keith countered. "And you're in a foreign country; you'll never get her out of Ireland." Nancy had to admire Keith's coolness in a hostage situation.

"Maybe not alive," Smithson sneered. "But I don't care about that. My employers will pay me, anyway. They aren't in this for the ransom money."

"What are they in it for, then?" Keith asked.

"To hurt Jacob Selkirk," Smithson snorted. "The way he shut down their business, with his stickybeak reporters prying into everything."

So it was the Australian crime ring who'd hired Smithson! Rachel was just a pawn in some pretty desperate dealings.

Nancy clutched the doorknob and gave the door a gentle shove. It wouldn't budge. She suspected she could break the rusty lock open, but not without making a lot of noise.

As if on cue, noise arrived—a thin whine in the distance, growing rapidly louder. A police helicopter, its searchlights raking the vast stretch of bog behind the house, was approaching. Keith's backup!

"We're closing in, Smithson," Keith shouted over the chopper's roar. "Hand her over peaceably, and it'll make things easier for you."

The noise was loud enough now to hide the sound of Nancy's movements. She shoved the door again with both hands and one strong foot. It wrenched open. She squeezed through into a small paneled entryway, and pushed through a dark passageway to her left, toward where Smithson and Rachel must be.

She couldn't hear Keith's next words, but Smithson's gruff answer was audible enough. Nancy used the sound to guide her along this narrow, windowless servants' passage. "It's great that the money's on its way," Smithson was saying. "But after I get it, I might do her in, anyway. My bosses have given me what they call 'discretion to do as I please.' Maybe I'll cut off her finger, like someone did to me. Would you like that, eh, miss?"

Getting closer now, Nancy heard a muffled, frightened yelp from Rachel, followed by Smithson's ugly laugh.

"Your daddo didn't treat me too well when I was working for him," the kidnapper snarled. "I don't owe him no favors."

His voice was directly behind the door next to Nancy.

Now she could hear Mulryan's voice outside, shouting, "Hurt the girl, and it won't look good at your trial." There was an edge of fear to his voice now. "Did you think of that, Smithson?"

Nancy drew a deep breath and thrust open the door.

Smithson, taken by surprise, wheeled around. He swung his gun toward Nancy.

Somehow in the sudden motion Rachel was able to wrestle out of Smithson's grasp. He lurched after her, lowering his gun for a moment. Nancy leaped toward him. With a karate chop, she knocked the weapon out of his right hand.

With an enraged roar, Smithson threw himself at Nancy. His left hand, with the stump where his little finger should be, flailed in front of her face. He tackled her, knocking her to the floor.

Rachel launched herself at Smithson from behind, her face contorted with fury. "How dare you do this to my father!" she screamed, raining blows on his back with her fists.

Garda officers came swarming in through the window and the passageway door. It took three of them to pull Smithson up off of Nancy. She shook her head to clear her senses. A hand reached down to help her to her feet.

Rachel grinned down at her. "Nancy—I've never been so happy to see anybody in my life!"

Lying in a four-poster bed at the old monastery, Nancy thought she was dreaming, hearing the chop of a speedboat outside her window. Was she reliving last night's adventure?

But now there was sunlight streaming through the arched stone window. When Nancy got up and looked out, there was the Garda speedboat again, with Keith Mulryan standing at the stern. But next to him was an unfamiliar figure: a stout man of about sixty, in an overcoat that looked like expensive cashmere. Though his hair was gray, something about his rugged features told her he was Rachel and Rhonda's father.

Nancy quickly threw on some jeans and a sweater and hurried downstairs. Hotel staff seemed to be rushing about everywhere, bringing trays of coffee and breakfast food into the lounge. Nancy strolled in to find the entire tour group settled on sofas and chairs, gazing wide-eyed at the famous tycoon. He sat ensconced in a throne-like leather wingback chair.

"Nancy!" Bob called out, seeing her. "We didn't want to wake you; you had such a hard night last night. As you can see, we've abandoned cycling for today. Too much other excitement."

The man in the wingback chair looked up. "Is this the same Nancy who is the hero of last night's crime scene?"

Rachel, perched beside him, jumped up. "Nancy, this is my dad."

"So I guessed." Nancy smiled and shook Jacob Selkirk's hand.

"I flew in from London as soon as I could after I received Smithson's ransom note," Selkirk said.

Rhonda, sitting on a footstool by his feet, looked concerned. "But, Dad—your busy schedule!"

Selkirk waved a hand. "How important are all those meetings, really? I had a daughter to rescue." He circled an arm around Rachel's waist and gave her a squeeze. "But I see she's already safe and sound."

Officer Mulryan smiled. "And Stewart Smithson is safely behind bars," he reported. "They're keeping him in the Galway jail to await trial. By the way, we'll have to take statements from all of you later today, to use as evidence."

"The hospital in Galway called a little while ago," Bob added. "The word is that Terry is resting comfortably. X rays showed he had a pretty bad concussion, but nothing more."

Mrs. Keenan, the innkeeper, sidled into the room, carrying a tall stack of newspapers. "Mr. Selkirk, sir," she said with a little bow, "here are all the papers your assistant sent over."

Carl Thompson whistled. "You read that many newspapers every morning?"

Jacob Selkirk chuckled. "I am in the business, you know. But I requested these papers today because they all have one thing in common: Rachel's kidnapping is on the front page."

Nancy was impressed. Stewart Smithson had been arrested last night at nearly ten P.M. How could so many reporters dig up enough information to produce a story for this morning's edition?

Jacob Selkirk fanned out the newspapers on the coffee table and let everyone in the group choose one. Bess was quick to snatch up the *London Enquirer.* "I found Derek's story," she called out. "Page nineteen.

Here's the headline: 'Irish Tourism Booms with Step-dancing Craze.'"

Camilla clapped for joy. "A fluffy travel piece—not what his editor expected. Derek will probably get sacked. But I knew he didn't have it in him to be too sleazy."

"Derek left the tour a day too soon," Bess declared. "He might have had a cover story after all."

Selkirk looked up. "Derek? Who's that?"

Rhonda slapped her dad's shoulder. "A reporter you fired once."

Selkirk shrugged. "There're lots of those around, dear."

Rachel smiled. "I'll tell you the whole story later, Dad. But Derek's really not cut out for the tabloids. Maybe you can find a spot for him on the *Clarion* again."

The phone out in the lobby jangled, and Mrs. Keenan trotted out. A moment later, she returned. "That was the Cashkellmara bike shop, Bob," she said. "Miss Selkirk's bike is fixed."

"Her bike?" Rhonda looked at her sister.

Mulryan nodded. "We took it in. It was terribly banged up when we found it. Smithson rammed it pretty hard into his trunk."

Rachel shuddered. "That must have been after he knocked me out. I put up a real fight when he ran me off my bike."

Jacob Selkirk smiled proudly. "That's my girl."

"I guess he knew he couldn't just leave the bike by the roadside," Mulryan said. "We'd be sure to spot it and know she'd been abducted."

Nancy nodded. "His whole plan depended on buying time. That's why he disabled Terry's van; Terry had just seen Rachel riding up ahead and was sure to report it."

"Time was of the essence," Mulryan agreed. "If we had waited until this morning to hunt for him, he'd have been long gone."

Rhonda closed her eyes. "What a horrible man. To think he used to drive us to school."

Selkirk reached over and patted her knee. "If I'd known, sweetie, I'd never have hired him. He's full of smooth talk when you first meet him, sure enough. By the time I'd realized what a crook he was, I'd fired him—but unfortunately, that just gave him a grudge. Made him fair game for my enemies to use."

Rachel, snuggled next to her father, made a face. "Well, I'm in no hurry to retrieve that bike. I don't intend to go cycling anytime soon."

Rhonda sat up, surprised. "What?"

Rachel paused and waggled one mischievous red eyebrow. "Not unless I've got a bodyguard riding right beside me. Any chance you'd be interested in the job, Nancy Drew?"